Praise for The Dirt Diary

"Holy fried onion rings! Fun from beginning to end."
—Wendy Mass, *New York Times* bestselling
author of *11 Birthdays* and *The Candymakers*

"I LOVED it…sweet, sensitive, and delicious!"
—Erin Dionne, author of
Models Don't Eat Chocolate Cookies

"Confidently addressing a number of common tween
troubles that include bullying, parental divorce, and
peer pressure, Staniszewski introduces a determined
eighth-grader desperate to get her separated parents back
together in this humorous problem novel."
—*Publishers Weekly*

"[An] appealing series that promises more goofball
humor blended with the real issues of early adolescence."
—*Booklist*

Praise for the My Very UnFairy Tale Life Series

"Anna Staniszewski creates a magical world that's totally relatable. You'll find yourself wishing you were alongside Jenny fighting against unicorns (who aren't as peaceful as you think) and traveling to fantastical realms."

—GirlsLife.com

"A light comic romp… Charming."

—*Kirkus*

"Staniszewski's debut is a speedy and amusing ride that displays a confident, on-the-mark brand of humor…will keep readers entertained."

—*Publishers Weekly*

"[A] breezy magical romp…the joking tone and thoughtful fairy tale play make this a fresh middle-grade read.

—Horn Book online

More great reads
by Anna Staniszewski

The Dirt Diary

My Very UnFairy Tale Life

My Epic Fairy Tale Fail

My Sort of Fairy Tale Ending

the
prank
list

Anna Staniszewski

sourcebooks
jabberwocky

Copyright © 2014 by Anna Staniszewski
Cover and internal design © 2014 by Sourcebooks, Inc.
Cover design by Regina Flath
Cover image by Michael Heath/Shannon and Associates

Sourcebooks and the colophon are registered trademarks of Sourcebooks, Inc.

Published by Sourcebooks Jabberwocky, an imprint of Sourcebooks, Inc.
P.O. Box 4410, Naperville, Illinois 60567-4410
(630) 961-3900
Fax: (630) 961-2168
www.jabberwockykids.com

Library of Congress Cataloging-in-Publication data is on file with the publisher.

Source of Production: Versa Press-USA, East Peoria, IL
Date of Production: May 2014
Run Number: 5001597

Printed and bound in the United States of America.
VP 10 9 8 7 6 5 4 3 2 1

For anyone who's ever felt like a piece of dirt.

Chapter 1

Rachel, stop holding your spatula like a knife!" Chef Ryan yells across the room. "How many times do I have to tell you?"

I change my grip on the spatula and keep stabbing at the pastries in front of me, imagining they're Chef Ryan's face. It's the first day of class at Ryan's Bakery, and already the owner hates me. For no reason.

Okay, maybe for a small reason.

I did spill flour all over the floor. Then I accidentally inhaled some of it and had a coughing fit that made me bump into a woman holding a pot of caramel. It splattered on top of the layer of flour, making an even more disgusting mess that stuck to everyone's shoes. So my first twenty minutes of class were spent mopping the floor while everyone else learned important tips on how to make today's assignment, tips that I totally missed, and now my batch of caramel squares has turned into a pan of goo on one side and crunchy crystals on the other.

Chef Ryan marches over to check out my sugar-tastrophe and sighs. Then he takes the spatula from me. "Watch," he says, separating the squares like he's done it a million times. "See? It's like cutting a sushi roll."

Since I don't want to get even more on his bad side, I stop myself from pointing out that I'm half Korean, *not* Japanese. Instead, I nod and give it another try.

"I don't care if you're a beginner or an expert!" Chef Ryan calls out to everyone as he finally leaves me alone. "This class may be called 'Pastries 101,' but I expect you all to be pros at learning!" He zeroes in on a stooped old man at the next table who seems afraid of his oven mitts.

Maybe one reason Chef Ryan hates me so much is because I'm the youngest person in his class. Not a lot of kids who've just finished eighth grade know they want to be pastry chefs one day. Then again, not a lot of kids grow up making their parents read them cookbooks instead of bedtime stories.

Too bad I'm failing miserably at showing Chef Ryan that I know what I'm doing. The more I move the caramel squares around, the more they turn into brown lumps. Gross. A trained hamster could have done better.

I glance over to make sure Chef Ryan isn't watching, and then I go back to holding the spatula *my* way. Much better. I might be self-taught, but that doesn't make me a total idiot in the kitchen.

I give the cookie sheet another stab with the spatula—and the whole thing flies off the counter and shoots across the room. It hits the wall and clatters to the floor. The brown lumps, though, stay stuck to the wall like muddy spitballs.

"Crabgrass!" I cry, letting loose one of Dad's goofy fake swear words.

"Rachel!" Chef Ryan hollers across the kitchen. Funny how of the twelve students in the class, I'm the only one whose name he knows so far.

As I run over to clean up the mess I've made—again— the door to the kitchen swings open.

I glance up and almost drop my dish towel at the sight of a boy about my age standing in the doorway. Oh my goldfish. He's tall and dark and handsome and every other cliché I can think of. (But he's not nearly as cute as Evan Riley. *My* Evan Riley.) He's also wearing a black leather jacket even though it's the middle of June.

Chef Ryan grimaces like he's caught a whiff of burned popcorn. "Can I help you?"

"Sorry I'm late," the boy says with a shrug. "I'm Whit."

"Whit?" Chef Ryan glances at his list. "I don't have you on here."

"It's Adam Whitney, but everyone calls me Whit."

Chef Ryan sighs like he's disappointed not to have an excuse to kick the boy out. "Class is more than half over. You can watch for the rest of today and take part next week. And be on time. I know you paid to take this class, but that doesn't mean I cater to you."

I can't help letting out a snort-laugh at the word "cater," the perfect baking pun. My dad would love it.

Chef Ryan shoots me a dirty look and turns back to Whit. "Go help Rachel clean up," he says. Then he walks away to check on other people. As he tests batter consistency and demonstrates proper pan-greasing techniques, I can't help noticing how much more patient he is with everyone else in the class than he is with me.

Whit hangs his leather jacket on a hook by the door and then pulls an apron on over his T-shirt and jeans. I guess he wants to look the part even though he won't actually be cooking. I wonder if he's new in town. Even if he's a little older than me, I'm sure I'd remember seeing him around.

Suddenly, I realize that I'm not cleaning anymore. In

fact, I'm just staring at Whit, watching his every move like he's the star of a cooking show. *Eek!* I snap my eyes away and go back to scrubbing the wall.

"What happened here?" Whit says, coming up beside me.

I clear my throat and manage to choke out: "A fatal baking accident."

He doesn't even crack a smile. Instead, he grabs a rag and starts de-gunking the wall along with me. Even though this mess is my doing, I don't object to having some help. There's only half an hour of class left, and at this rate, I'll be doing more scrubbing than cooking. I didn't talk my mom into letting me out of cleaning houses on Saturday mornings for the next few weeks so I could spend the time cleaning anyway.

"Okay!" Chef Ryan calls out. "Let's move on to making a chocolate glaze to serve with your caramel squares."

Chocolate glaze? I know how to make that. I've made it a dozen times. Finally, this is my chance to prove to Chef Ryan that I'm not a moron. I start scrubbing furiously, but that just makes the rag shoot out of my hand.

What is wrong with me? Do I have springs in my fingers today?

Whit gives me a pitying look, like I'm a sick poodle that can't help being pathetic.

As I go to the window to grab the rag off the floor, I notice a red and black van driving by with the words "Ladybug Cleaners" painted on the side. Directly behind it are another and another, like a swarm of ladybug minivans leaving their nest.

What the Shrek?

Mom and I have run into other cleaning businesses in the area, but none have looked so professional. And none have reminded me of a horde of insects about to take over the whole town.

Suddenly, the chocolate glaze doesn't seem important anymore. I tell myself I'm being crazy-face. It's only one competitor. There's plenty of room for all of us. But ever since Dad left, the cleaning business has been the only reason Mom and I have been able to stay in our house.

My family already imploded over the past year. I *cannot* deal with anything else changing.

Chapter 2

How was class?" Mom asks as I hop into her dented minivan. I'm supposed to help her with the rest of the day's cleaning jobs, so we head to one of the fancy housing developments on the other side of town, the kind with mansions so big that they make our house look like a stick of gum.

"Good." I force myself to smile. After how excited I was about this class, I don't want to let on what a disappointment the first day was. Not when Mom is finally starting to accept that my love of baking is more than a hobby that distracts me from my schoolwork. "We made caramel squares."

"Yum!" she says. "Did you get to bring any home?"

"Um, no." I cringe as I remember the awful feeling of having to dump the whole batch in the trash. I bet even the garbage can was grossed out by my handiwork. "Maybe next time."

I'm determined to practice all week so that I can make a better impression on Chef Ryan next Saturday. I miss Ms. Kennedy, my middle-school home ec teacher. She's always been so encouraging about my baking. I've never had to prove myself to her. But clearly not all food people are like that. Chef Ryan might hate me now, but I have six weeks to change his mind.

"By the way, we have one less stop this afternoon," Mom says as we pull up to Andrew Ivanoff's house. "Mr. Jacobs said he'll be out of town on business for the summer, so he's closing up the house."

I'm barely listening as I glance down the street toward where Marisol lives. My best friend is probably in her room right now, surrounded by pieces of fabric, creating some amazing new outfit. It's totally bizarro that, meanwhile, I'm about to go clean her boyfriend's house. Not that I'll actually see him. Andrew is off at film camp for the whole summer, which you'd think would make Marisol upset, but she says being apart will give her more time to be creative. She's a much stronger person than I am. If Evan left for the summer, I'd probably be moping around the whole time.

"Rachel?" Mom says.

I blink, realizing I'm standing outside the Ivanoffs' house with a broom under one arm and furniture polish under the other. Whenever I start thinking about Evan, time seems to ooze by.

Once my brain starts working normally again, we zip through the Ivanoffs' house and clean our way across the neighborhood, battling dirty underwear, scummy bathtubs, and mysterious clumps of smelliness that make me wish I owned a gas mask. Just think, then I could be the Gas-Masked Crusader (aka the worst superhero ever).

When we get back into the car, I'm sweating like crazy. Most of the houses we clean have central air, but scrubbing toilets during the summer is still gross. I'm panting in front of the car air vent and wiping my face with a paper towel when I notice it: a Ladybug Cleaners van sitting outside Mr. Jacobs' house.

Two women in red and black aprons pile out of the van and start bustling around, bringing supplies inside. They look like efficient cleaning robots. No dropping mops or tripping over vacuum cleaner cords like I'm always doing. Why haven't I seen them around town before? How could a whole cleaning service appear out of nowhere?

"Mom, didn't you say that Mr. Jacobs was out of town?"

"Yes, why?" She must not have noticed the van as we drove by.

"No reason," I say, but my pulse is fluttering. This can't be good.

"All right," Mom says, pulling onto Main Street, "off to our last stop."

I try to shake the uneasy feeling in my chest. We have lots of loyal clients. Even if we lose one or two to the Ladybugs, we'll be fine. There's no need to tell Mom about it. She's got enough permanent worry lines on her face as it is.

Our last stop of the day, Caitlin Schubert's house, is nothing like the fancy monstrosities we usually clean. It's a normal ranch-style house with a normal lawn. No moat or anything. I used to hate being anywhere near Caitlin, but things have changed a lot the past few months. I don't think we'll ever be friends, but at least I don't feel like a piece of belly-button lint around her anymore.

When Caitlin's mother, Ms. Montelle, opens the door for us, she's excited to see us as usual. Since talking to people has never been my thing, I don't mind that most of our clients act like we're invisible, but it's still nice to be treated like an actual human once in a while.

Caitlin is away visiting relatives, so for once I can go into her room without fearing for my life. As I finish dusting the dresser, I spot a silver necklace in Caitlin's open jewelry box that I used to see her wearing all the time. Hanging from the chain is half of a full-moon charm. Briana Riley (Evan's evil twin sister) has the other half, though I have no idea if she still wears it, especially now that she and Caitlin aren't BFFs anymore.

I can't help running my fingers over the necklace. It feels like a symbol of everything that happened at the end of eighth grade: me winning the bake sale; Mom and me getting closer; Marisol and Andrew getting together; and— most importantly—Evan and me patching things up. It boggles my mind how different things are now than they were a few weeks ago.

"Rachel?"

I glance up to find Ms. Montelle peering at me from the doorway. I realize I'm still clutching Caitlin's necklace. It slips through my fingers and falls back into Caitlin's jewelry box.

"Sorry," I say, my cheeks suddenly hot. "I swear I wasn't snooping." I definitely learned my lesson about *that* at the end of eighth grade. "The necklace…it was just…I'm surprised Caitlin didn't take it with her."

Ms. Montelle nods slowly. "She never used to take it off. She says the clasp is broken, but I'm not sure that's the whole reason she stopped wearing it." She sighs. "I guess a lot has changed recently. For all of us."

I nod. I've never been good with change. I mean, hello, I stole money from my college fund to fly down to Florida and try to talk my dad into coming home, all in a desperate attempt to get my life back to how it used to be.

"How are you doing with everything?" Ms. Montelle says, giving me a searching look.

"I'm fine," I say. And even though it sounds weird to admit it—how can I be okay when my dad isn't around anymore?—it feels true. Maybe I'm better with change than I thought.

Or maybe I'm good at lying to myself.

Chapter 3

When the doorbell rings the next day, I have clumps of caramel in my hair and a thick layer of flour on my apron. Mom is out on a lunch date with Mr. Hammond (her new boyfriend and my middle-school vice principal— how's that for awkward?), so I asked Evan to come watch our favorite show, *Pastry Wars*, and do some baking.

"Whoa," he says when he sees me. "Looks like you started without me." His green eyes twinkle at me with amusement.

"Sorry. I was trying to figure out these caramel squares." Just then, the timer goes off, meaning the squares are ready. I hold my breath as I go to take them out of the oven, hoping they come out less horrible than the ones I made in pastry class. I pull open the oven door and gasp.

"Wow," Evan says, coming up beside me. "Those look awesome."

"They really do," I say as I put them on the counter. I

can practically hear angels singing up in baking heaven. "Why couldn't I do that yesterday?"

"Why, what happened yesterday?"

As we wait for the squares to cool, I tell Evan about the disastrous first day of class.

"You had an off day," he says when I'm finished. "Happens to the best of us."

"I hope you're right." Maybe I was just nervous and that's why I messed up every single step. I grab a spatula and quickly cut up the squares, doing it my usual way instead of the weird way Chef Ryan showed me. This time it works fine. Finally, I grab a gooey piece and place it on my tongue. "Mmmm." It's amazing, if I do say so myself.

"These are amazing," Evan says after he's swallowed a bite. I guess it's unanimous.

"That'll show Chef Ryan and Whit," I say.

"Who's Whit?" Evan asks, popping another bite of caramel square into his mouth.

I sigh. "This guy in my class. He was my partner yesterday, and he probably thinks all I'm good at is making a mess. Next week I'm going to wow him and everyone else with my super-incredible baking skills."

Evan gives me his trademark crooked grin. "They're definitely incredible."

Could he be any cuter? I practically float over to the couch. "Which episode do you want to watch?" We've both seen every episode of *Pastry Wars* ever made, which is one of the things that first helped us get to know each other. If we hadn't had that icebreaker, I probably would have been too scared to talk to him.

"Whichever one you want, Booger Crap." He flashes a smile as I roll my eyes at the goofy fake swear turned nickname. "It doesn't really matter as long as we get to watch it together."

My heart starts flopping in my chest like a fish. When he says things like that, I have no doubt that he really likes me. Even if he hasn't called me his girlfriend yet, he must think of me that way. As far as I know, he's not hanging out with any other girls.

I wish I could ask him about it, but I think my tongue would turn black and fall out if I even tried. So, instead, I turn on the first episode I find and tell myself to calm down.

"What's wrong?" Evan says after a minute.

"Huh?" I realize that instead of looking at the TV, I've been staring at his profile. Honestly, sometimes I think my body and my brain aren't even connected.

"Are you okay?"

"Yeah…I was…" *Do it*, a little voice in the back of my brain says, one that sounds suspiciously like my best friend, Marisol. *Just ask him if he thinks of you as his girlfriend. At least then you'll know.* Maybe my internal Marisol is right, and I do need to come out and ask him. I open my mouth, excited and terrified at the idea that I might actually manage to spit out the words, when—

Riiing!

I jump at the sound of the house phone. As I rush over to pick it up, I wonder if it's a sign that asking Evan about our relationship is a bad idea. Maybe it would scare him away.

"Hello?"

"Hi, Rachel," a woman's voice says on the other end. "It's Linda Montelle."

"Oh, hi. My mom's not home right now, but you can try her cell phone if you need—"

"Actually, you're the one I was looking for. I was hoping you could help me. I was planning to take Caitlin's necklace in to the jeweler to be fixed. You know, the one you and I were talking about yesterday? But I can't seem to find it."

"I'm pretty sure I put it back in her jewelry box."

"I thought so, too," she says. "Maybe it fell behind the dresser. Sometimes, I think we must have fairies living in this house!" She lets out a light laugh. "Anyway, I thought I'd check with you first before I started moving furniture around."

My brain is spinning. I *did* put the necklace back right where I found it, didn't I? "I can help you look for it when we're there next week, if you want," I offer.

"That's all right. In fact, I forgot to tell your mom that I'll be out of town next weekend so you two don't have to worry about stopping by. I'll be in touch with her to set up another time, okay?"

"Oh. Okay, I'll let her know."

I slowly put the phone down after she's hung up, still racking my brain. I swear I put the necklace right back in the box. Unless there was an earthquake last night—one that only hit underneath Caitlin's house—I don't know how it could have fallen out.

Ms. Montelle was acting like it wasn't a big deal, but what if her suddenly not wanting us to come by next week means that she blames me for the necklace going missing? No way. I'm being a paranoid panther. Ms. Montelle has been our most loyal client from the beginning. Her canceling on us next week is just a coincidence. It has to be.

Chapter 4

When I was younger, Mom would ship me off to camp for the summer where I'd be forced to weave ugly, lopsided baskets and half drown in a swampy lake. Thankfully, those days are over. Now Mom drops me off at Marisol's house on her way to her office job so she doesn't have to worry about me spending the whole day by myself.

When I get to Marisol's, her mom lets me in and then promptly goes back to her laptop. She's a freelance writer, which means she spends most of the day in sweatpants, furiously typing away. It drives Marisol nuts that her mom is always home because she gets almost no privacy. I have to admit that the whole thing makes me a little jealous. Now that my mom and I are getting along better, I wish she were home more often.

Ever since school ended, Marisol's been painting a mural on her wall, so her bedroom is particularly chaotic when I go in. One end of the room is draped with sheets, and there are fans going in all the windows. She only has one corner of the mural done so far, but I can already tell it's going to be amazing.

"What's that?" I say, peering at the newest sketch she's added near her closet. One of the people looks hunched and bloody. "Wait! It's a zombie, isn't it?"

She smiles. "How'd you guess?"

"Oh, I don't know. Maybe because your boyfriend is obsessed with the undead?"

Marisol's eyes widen, and she rushes over to shut the door to her room. "We have to be careful about using that word, remember?" she whispers. "My mom is right downstairs."

"Sorry!" I whisper back. Marisol's mom thinks she should wait until she's older to start dating, so her relationship with Andrew has been top secret. "Has she ever met him?"

Marisol shakes her head. "Not yet. You know how weird she is about me even having friends who are guys."

"You should have Andrew come over so your mom can see how nice he is. Then she might not care that you two are together."

"Maybe when he gets home from camp in a few weeks, I'll give it a try." She sighs and shoves a paintbrush in my hand. I'm not good at making actual art, but I'm not bad at filling in the parts that Marisol tells me to. "You're so lucky that your mom is okay with you having a boyfriend."

I sigh right back as I start painting a patch of grass near the zombie's feet. "He's not my boyfriend."

"Of course he is! Even if you guys haven't had 'The Talk' yet, that doesn't mean anything. There isn't anyone else you're interested in, right?"

For some bizarre reason, I think of Whit from my pastry class.

"Rachel?" Marisol's eyebrows shoot up. "Is there another guy I don't know about?" She gasps. "You're not still stuck on Steve Mueller, are you?"

"No!" I might have been obsessed with Steve Mueller for most of eighth grade, but Evan is a million times better than him. Besides, after Steve dumped Briana Riley, he started dating Caitlin Schubert. They're kind of perfect for each other, which makes me especially glad I'm finally over him. "It's nothing…I mean, no one. I was just…"

Unfortunately, Marisol can always see right through me. "Who is he?"

I shake my head. "It's really nothing. There's this guy in my pastry class. He's cute and everything, but I'm not interested in him at all. He's too…" I can't even find the words. Whit might be cute, but I didn't get the friendliest vibe from him the other day. Besides, he's not my type. Evan Riley is my type, plain and simple. "I guess meeting him got me thinking about what would happen if he asked me out on a date or something. I couldn't say I had a boyfriend because I don't, not technically."

Marisol laughs. "Look at you. Remember two months ago when you were convinced no guy could ever like you? And now you're worried about having too many of them swooning at your feet."

My cheeks start to burn. "Shut up!" I say, threatening her with my paintbrush. I know she's joking, but for some reason it still embarrasses me. I'm definitely not over the shock of Evan actually liking me. Maybe that's why this whole boyfriend thing has been worrying me so much. "Anyway, we haven't even held hands yet or anything."

Marisol waggles her dark eyebrows. "Maybe not yet, but wait until he kisses you."

My face is suddenly so hot that I have to go stand in front of one of the fans to cool down. Just as I'm starting to feel better, I spot a Ladybug Cleaners van driving by. I press my face to the window and watch it stop outside Angela Bareli's house next door.

"Holy poached pears!" I cry.

"What's wrong?"

I quickly tell Marisol about the new cleaning business in town. Together, we watch as two identically dressed women pile out of the van and go into the Barelis' house. Considering that Mrs. Bareli is in my mom's book club, it's kind of an insult that she wouldn't hire us to clean for her.

"I bet Angela convinced her mom to get someone else," I say. "She probably hates me for winning the bake sale this year."

"She might still be mad about that, but she should be thanking you for finally making Briana Riley all hers." Marisol rolls her eyes. "Now that Briana and Caitlin aren't friends anymore, Angela can't stop talking about how she and Briana are 'the bestest besties.' I'm waiting for them to get matching tattoos or something."

I try to laugh, but I'm still staring at the Ladybug Cleaners van. What do they have that we don't?

"I'm pretty sure Mr. Jacobs lied to us about being out

of town," I say. "He wanted the Ladybug people to do his house instead. Do you think they're better than us?"

"Definitely not better," Marisol says in the reassuring tone she uses when she thinks I'm taking things way too seriously. "But is it possible they're cheaper?"

"I—I don't know. My mom based her prices on the other places in town, but maybe they're charging less." I shake my head. "We can't compete with that. If we charge any less than we already do, we'll barely be able to pay for the gas to drive around town."

Suddenly, I'm gasping for air. After Dad left, my whole world felt like it was falling apart. If anything else goes wrong…

"Rachel, relax," says Marisol, clearly noticing that I'm about to hyperventilate. "It'll be fine."

"What if we have to move out of town?" I say, still wheezing. Is this what a panic attack feels like? "I can't leave you and Evan and—"

"I know, but you guys will figure it out." Marisol gives my hand a squeeze. "And I'll help you, okay? Whatever it takes."

I nod, finally able to suck in a breath. "Whatever it takes."

Chapter 5

When pastry class rolls around again on Saturday morning, I'm ready. I've been practicing all week, and I'm determined to impress Chef Ryan.

Except he's not there.

Instead, a woman I don't recognize greets us with a smile, her short curls bouncing like they're made out of Slinkies.

"Hi, everyone!" she says. "My name's Cherie. I'm Chef Ryan's wife. He's a little under the weather, so I'll be taking over the class today." Something about the way she blinks while she's talking makes me think that she's not being totally honest. Maybe Chef Ryan couldn't deal with another session of watching me accidentally destroy his kitchen.

"We'll be making chocolate chip cookies," she announces.

I stifle a groan while everyone else around me perks up. I guess they're excited to make something easy, but I've been making chocolate chip cookies from scratch since I was a little kid. The whole reason I wanted to take this class was so I could push myself to make things I might not be brave enough to try on my own.

Whit lets out a grunt beside me. Maybe he's not thrilled about making something easy, either. Or he's part gorilla.

"Let's get in pairs so we can help each other," Cherie calls out.

People start to team up while I stand in the corner having traumatizing flashbacks to gym class. Finally, I glance over at Whit and realize he's the only one without a partner. I guess that means he has no choice but to work with me.

He seems to realize the same thing because he comes over and hands me the recipe Cherie passed out to us.

"I'll take the lead," he says, as if it's obvious that he'll be the one in charge. I'm tempted to argue, but I figure it's not worth it. Since Chef Ryan isn't here, there's no one for me to impress anyway.

Whit goes to gather the ingredients while I bring over the pans we'll need. A sinking feeling keeps growing in my stomach. I've been looking forward to taking a pastry class for so long, and so far it's been one huge disappointment.

"Rachel," Cherie says, coming over to me. "My husband said you were having some trouble last week."

Great. And now I've been labeled the dunce in the class.

"I was having an off day," I say. I can practically hear Whit listening to our conversation as he stands behind me.

She smiles brightly, obviously humoring me. "Well, if you need any help, I'm right here. I'm not as skilled as my husband, but I'm not bad."

"Is he really sick?" Whit asks over my shoulder.

Cherie's smile fades. "No…not exactly." She looks around and then lowers her voice. "The truth is, I'm the one who talked him into doing this class, hoping it would bring in more business. My husband loves being in the kitchen, but talking to people…" She laughs. "That's more my department."

Now that's something I can understand. I'm always much better in the kitchen by myself than with other people around. If I had to teach a cooking class, I'd probably hate every minute of it, too.

"Okay, I'll stop distracting you!" Cherie chirps before going to check on Mr. Leroy, the little old man who was having even more trouble last week than I was. He looks just as nervous today, but at least he's teamed up with a middle-aged woman who has a patient, kindergarten-teacher smile constantly plastered on her face.

The Prank List

Whit and I get to work, and after only a minute, I already want to smack him. He keeps reading the instructions aloud and then stopping to explain every step to me, like I'm a two-year-old. Clearly, he thinks he's too good for this class and too good to be working with a klutz like me. I wonder why he's here in the first place since he seems convinced he already knows everything.

"You're doing that wrong," he says, after we've made our dough and he's "letting me" scoop it onto the cookie sheet. How did I ever think he was cute? He's one of the most annoying people I've ever met.

"What are you talking about?" I say. And then, because I can't take it anymore, I add, "I've baked chocolate chip cookies a million and a half times in the past few years. Trust me, I know what I'm doing."

He ignores me and says, "If you make the cookies smaller, they come out better. Watch." He grabs the spoon from me and starts dishing out tiny scoops of dough, like he's making cookies for a little-kid tea party.

"Fine," I say. "We'll do half your way and half my way." Then he'll see that my way is better.

He smirks, and I have a feeling he's thinking the same thing. "Fine."

When our cookie sheet is filled, we put it in the oven. I realize we're done before anyone else in the class, so now all there is to do is wait.

The silence between us grows and grows until it's an eight-legged monster. The fact that Whit's a total snob doesn't make me all that eager to get chummy with him, but the silence is so thick now that I'm afraid it'll clog my lungs.

"So," I finally say, determined to make conversation like a normal person, "what grade are you in?"

"Going into ninth," he says.

"Me too. Did you just move to town?"

He shakes his head. "I live in Plainville, but when I found out that this place had a pastry class, I convinced my sister to drop me off on her way to work."

"Oh," I say. More silence. *Think, Rachel. What would Mom say in this situation?* "So your sister is older?"

"Yeah, I live with her and her family," he says, playing with the strings of his apron. "That's why I'm here. I already know all this stuff, of course, but if I can say I've taken some classes, it'll help me get a job at a bakery. Then I can help my sister out with paying the bills."

Suddenly, my hatred for Whit is a little less intense.

Helping your family is something I can definitely understand. I want to tell him about working with my mom, but instead I find myself blurting out: "I don't have a sister. Or a brother. I had a guinea pig once, but that doesn't really count." Wow, my conversational skills keep getting better and better. "Do your parents live with your sister, too?" There, that's a normal thing to ask.

His face darkens. "My mom's having a rough time right now and my dad died a few years ago, so my sister and her husband took me in."

"Oh, I–I'm…" Luckily, the timer goes off, saving me from sticking my foot even further into my mouth. Whit and I hurry over to take out the cookie sheets and put them on the counter to cool.

"Those look great," Cherie calls to us. "But why are they two different sizes?"

Whit and I exchange looks. "Hey, Cherie," he calls back. "Can you do a taste test for us?"

Her face lights up as she bounces over to us. "Of course."

She tastes one of Whit's tiny cookies and one of my normal-sized ones. As she chews both carefully, like she's making an important decision, I'm dying from the suspense.

"Well?" I finally say.

"The smaller ones are cooked more evenly," she says slowly, "but they're a little dry." I'm about to let out a triumphant hoot when she continues: "And the bigger ones are nice and chewy, but they're a little underdone." She smiles at us. "So I think I'll have to call this one a tie."

I feel myself deflate while Whit's face goes boiling red. "Are you serious?" he says. "I know my stuff is better. My school did baking competitions all the time, and I always won."

"Sorry!" Cherie chirps. "I just call them like I see them!" Her brow furrows. "A baking competition? How does that work?"

I'm afraid Whit's anger might boil over like a pot of soup, but he seems to calm down enough to explain about the "bakefest" at his middle school. Kids would be given an hour to make an assigned recipe and then be judged in front of an audience. I have to admit that it sounds amazing.

"Wow! That's like something you'd see on TV," Cherie says. "We should do that here! I bet Chef Ryan would love it."

I give her a skeptical look.

Cherie laughs. "Okay, he might not love it. But I think

he'd like judging that kind of competition if I organized it. Maybe we could do a bake-off at the end of the class as a way to show off what you guys have learned. What do you think?"

"Sure," Whit says with a smug smile that I know means he's convinced he's going to win yet again.

"That sounds great," I say. Maybe the bake-off will finally give me a chance to prove myself to Chef Ryan. And to put Whit in his place.

I leave class smiling this time. As I go over to Mom's minivan, which is waiting for me on the corner, I spot a blur of red and black driving past. My smile fades as a Ladybug Cleaners van goes by, its engine buzzing like a big, ugly insect.

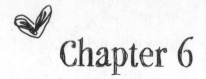

Chapter 6

O kay," Mom says as we get back into the car after a long afternoon of scrubbing, mopping, and vacuuming. "Since we don't have Ms. Montelle's house to do today, we're finished for the day."

"Did she ever call to reschedule?"

"Not yet, but I'm sure she will."

I swallow. "I hope so."

Mom gives me a sharp look. "Did something happen?"

"Um…" I don't want to tell her about the necklace, but I have no choice. When I'm done explaining what happened, I expect Mom to get all anxious about losing business. But weirdly, she just smiles. Mr. Hammond really has been a good influence on her. She's been so much more laid-back the past few weeks than…well, than I've ever seen her.

"I'm sure it's nothing to worry about, Rachel. She knows you would never take anything."

"But what if she can't find it? Won't I be the obvious person to blame since I was the last one to touch it?"

"Don't worry. It'll all work itself out."

I hope she's right, but I can't help stressing about it all the way home. What if Ms. Montelle not only blames me for the missing necklace but tells other people about it? We've already started losing cleaning jobs to the Ladybugs. We can't risk losing any more.

I'm still turning everything over in my brain after I get home and collapse on my bed. I do a halfhearted search online for the Ladybugs' cleaning prices, but I don't find anything useful. Exhausted, I curl up for a nap, but as soon as my head hits the pillow, my cell phone rings. It's Dad.

"Hey there, Rachel Roo," he says. "How's it hopping?"

"Fine," I say, flopping back on my bed. "We just got home from cleaning."

"Ah, look at you. A real career woman."

"I guess." I can't help being a little bitter. I may not be the only girl my age with a job, but most kids I know work for spending money, not for cash to help their moms pay the mortgage. Dad has been paying child support, but based on how worried Mom has been, I can tell it's not enough. Maybe if Dad was still living with us, things would be different…

I try to shake the thought out of my head. Dwelling on stuff like that doesn't do any good.

"Sooo," Dad says in a tone that means he's trying to be casual but that he's about to tell me something important. "I was thinking of coming up there soon."

I sit up on my bed, the tiredness suddenly gone. "You're coming to visit?" I haven't seen my dad in months! The thought of hugging him again makes tears prick at my eyes.

"Well, sort of," he says slowly. "It might be a visit. Or it might be a longer thing."

"Longer? You mean, you'd be staying up here?"

He lets out a whooshing breath. "Nothing's decided yet, but to be honest with you, the scuba business hasn't been going very well. I'd hate to give up on it, but I don't know if there's much of a future here."

"What about…what about your new girlfriend?"

"Ellie wants me to do whatever is right for me. She understands."

I guess that means Dad's relationship with her isn't all that serious. I can't help feeling relieved. Even if my parents are almost divorced, that doesn't mean I'm totally okay with the idea of them dating other people, even if those people are as nice as Mr. Hammond.

"Anyway," Dad goes on, "I'm still figuring things out. But maybe it's time for me to come home."

"Home? You mean, back to us? Back to…Mom?"

He sighs. "I shouldn't have said anything to you until I'd talked to her. I'm not even sure she'd take me back. Don't tell her about this, okay? Promise?"

I can't breathe. After all the time I spent trying to get my parents back together—and failing miserably—*now* my dad has suddenly changed his mind?

"I promise," I whisper. "But, Dad, what if it's too late?" Mom has finally started getting over the fact that Dad left. If he showed up on our doorstep, would it make her start psychotically labeling and organizing things again? I don't want to go back to unalphabetizing my bookshelves on a daily basis.

"It very well might be," he says, "but maybe it's worth a try. And once I was back, I'd find a steadier job up there and you two wouldn't have to work so hard anymore. I mean, the cleaning business was a good temporary solution, but it's nothing you gals would want to do long term, right?"

I'm not sure what to say to that. Cleaning toilets isn't exactly my lifelong ambition, but it hasn't been so bad. And I know Mom actually loves it. Her boss at the law office is okay, but he doesn't really respect her. At least with the cleaning business, she doesn't have to worry about all of that. I think she likes being the one in charge.

But I don't have time to explain all that to my dad because he gets a work call on the other line. "Sorry, Roo. I have to go. We'll talk about this later."

After we hang up the phone, my brain is throbbing. I should be happy. This is what I've wanted ever since Dad left—for him to miss us and realize that he can't live without us. But things are different now. If Dad came back, I'm not sure there would even be room for him in our lives.

Chapter 7

As I sleepily shovel cereal into my mouth on Monday morning, Mom paces around the house talking to someone on the phone. When she finally comes into the kitchen, her cheeks are bright pink.

"We just lost a client," she says, pushing her blond bangs away from her face.

"Who?" I say through a mouthful of Corn Flakes.

"Mrs. Vanguard down on Rowland Drive. I tried to convince her to stay with us, but she said she's found another service, Ladybug Cleaners, that can come in the mornings during the week. I guess they're new in the area."

As I gulp the last bite of cereal, it scratches my throat on the way down. I guess there's no hiding the Ladybugs from Mom anymore. "So that's it?" I say, coughing. "She's firing us?"

"We didn't do anything wrong, so I don't think you can

call it firing. We're just not a good fit. I can't exactly leave my day job to go clean her house in the mornings, now can I?" Mom sighs again and goes to pour herself some coffee.

Is it possible that Ms. Montelle told Mrs. Vanguard about the necklace and that's why she doesn't want us to clean her house anymore? I'm sure Mom would tell me it's a coincidence, but what if it's not?

"By the way," Mom calls over her shoulder, "I've asked a real-estate agent to come by this Wednesday to take a look at the house and see how much he thinks we could sell it for."

"What?" I drop my spoon into my cereal, sending a spray of milk up my nose.

"Now, don't panic. This doesn't mean anything. If all goes well, it won't come to that. But it's best to know what our options are, don't you think?"

All I can do is stare at her. I've lived in this house since I was three years old. I can't even imagine another option.

Mom puts her hand on my shoulder. "I know you love this place, Rachel. I do, too. There are so many..." She clears her throat. "There are so many memories here. I promise that I'll do everything I can to make sure we can stay."

I'm dying to tell Mom about my conversation with Dad last night. If she thinks there's a chance he might come home, will she stop thinking about selling the house?

But I can't tell her. Not only did I promise Dad that I wouldn't, but I have no idea how she might react. For all I know, she'd call Dad and forbid him from setting foot in our house again. The last thing I want to do is make things worse.

● ● ●

After Mom drops me off on her way to work the next day, I run up to Marisol's room, desperate to tell her about my conversation with my dad. Today, because it's too hot to add on to the mural, her room is covered with scraps of fabric and half-finished dresses.

Marisol shakes her head when I'm done telling her everything. "And I thought *my* family had a lot of drama. My brother setting our yard on fire is nothing compared to what you've been dealing with."

I glance out her bedroom window at the newly scorched grass behind the house. "Yeah, at least you guys put that fire out right away. I feel like all I've been doing since my dad left is running around with a fire extinguisher."

"I know what will cheer you up!" Marisol declares with a big grin. "Well, at least *I'm* excited about it."

"Did you make a new outfit?"

"Better!" She stands up in the middle of her room like she has an important announcement. "Remember how you were telling me about the bake-off idea? Well, I was thinking, what if it was a whole big event? So instead of just a baking competition, what if there was music and"—she bounces up and down—"a fashion show!"

I jump to my feet. "Marisol, that's perfect! Evan's talked about wanting to play a live show. Maybe he could even get a band together. And maybe—"

"You could be one of my models!"

My excitement turns into complete horror. "What are you talking about?"

"We'll get the people from your pastry class to model aprons or something. It'll be great!"

"No way. It's bad enough I'll have to bake in front of an audience. I'm not going to try to walk in a straight line in front of them. I'll totally stumble into an oven and bake myself to death by accident."

Marisol rolls her eyes. "Fine. Be a poopy head about it."

"Did you just call me a poopy head? What are we, five years old?"

She shrugs. "I call 'em like I see 'em."

Just then, her phone beeps. By the smile that lights up her face, I can tell it's a message from Andrew.

"How does he like film camp?" I ask.

"He says they're keeping him busy, but that he misses me." Her cheeks flush with obvious happiness as she sends him a message back.

I can't help feeling a stab of jealousy. Why can't the guy I like be clearer about how he feels?

For some reason, I find myself thinking about Whit and wondering if he's the kind of guy who would be weird about calling someone his girlfriend.

Ew! Why am I even thinking about that? Who cares about stuck-up Whit? He's the last person I would ever want to date.

I plop down in front of the AC, suspecting that my brain is overheating or something and that's why I'm having these ridiculous ideas. I need to relax and be patient, like Marisol's always telling me to be. Evan will have to come around eventually. Right?

Chapter 8

After an entire morning of planning the Bake-Off Extravaganza, Marisol and I brave the heat to bike over to Ryan's Bakery. I'm hoping Cherie will be there since she was so excited about the bake-off idea, but of course Chef Ryan is the one behind the counter instead.

"I'll be right with you," he calls when we go inside. He's hunched over a three-tiered wedding cake, dotting it with perfect icing flowers. When he's done, he smiles down at his work in satisfaction and then glances up at us. His smile fades when he sees me. "Oh, Rachel. What can I do for you?"

I swallow and blink at him a few times until Marisol elbows me in the ribs.

"Ouch!" Rubbing my side, I step forward and mumble: "Um, your wife seemed excited about doing a bake-off. I don't know if she told you, but it would be a competition at the end of our class where we'd kind of show off what we learned in front of an audience?" He just stares at me, so I have no idea if he knows what I'm talking about. "Um, well anyway, my friend here had this really good idea to make it into a big event, and, um…" I look to Marisol for help.

She flashes a confident smile. "You guys are pretty new in town, right? Well, this will be a great way to get publicity for your bakery!" she says. Then she goes on to explain her ideas, highlighting all the business the event will attract. "So what do you think?"

Chef Ryan wipes his hands on his apron and sighs. "I think it sounds like a lot of work, but Cherie's convinced the Bake-Off will bring in more business, so I guess it's happening, no matter what I say. Maybe making it a higher profile event will attract more people."

"We'll help plan it," Marisol assures him. "It'll be worth the trouble. I promise."

The bell on the door jingles, and we turn to see a pretty young woman with black hair come in. She's holding a toddler in her arms who's sucking on a stuffed animal and managing to make seagull-like sounds at the same time. I nearly fall over when I realize the woman is wearing a red apron with black dots on it. Holy twice-baked potatoes. She's one of the Ladybugs!

"What can I get you?" Chef Ryan calls to her, waving us aside. Clearly, he's tired of dealing with us.

"I wanted to get a cake for my husband's birthday," she says, shifting the baby to one hip so she can actually see Chef Ryan.

I turn to go, but Marisol grabs my arm. Her eyes are bright in an I-have-an-idea way that makes me nervous. She marches over to the woman and says: "Excuse me. You work for that new cleaning service, right?"

"I do," the woman says.

"Great. I was wondering if you could tell me your prices and stuff. My mom's been looking for a cleaning lady."

"Of course. Well, it all depends on the size of your house. If you—" The toddler lets out a deafening shriek, and the woman gives Marisol an apologetic smile. "Here," she says over her son's screams, riffling around in her pockets until she finds a business card. "Have your mom give me a call and we can figure out the details."

"Thanks!" Marisol calls as I pull her away and out of the bakery. Even when we're outside, I can still hear the toddler screaming.

"What was that about?" I say. "I thought you were all about being honest, no matter what. Remember how mad you got at me when I didn't tell you about spying on Briana because you were convinced that only horrible people lie?"

Marisol shrugs. "It wasn't a lie. My mom keeps talking about hiring a cleaning lady, but I don't think she'll ever actually do it. She would never let anyone see our house when it's not spotless." She looks over the Ladybug business card. "Wow, it says that woman is the owner."

"Really?" We glance back through the window as the lady bounces the toddler up and down and chats with Chef Ryan. "Funny, she doesn't look like she's made of pure evil."

Marisol rolls her eyes. "I guess sometimes it's hard to tell. Anyway, I'll try to convince my mom to call her. Maybe we can get some info that way."

"Wait," I say. "Maybe I should be the one to call. I can pretend to be your mom."

Marisol's mouth falls open in surprise. "You hate talking to people you don't know on the phone. Remember how long it took you to call me when we first became friends?"

"I know, but maybe I can get some more dirt on the Ladybugs this way."

Marisol purses her lips. "So you'd lie about being my mom?" I can tell she doesn't like the idea.

"I don't have to say your name or anything. It won't be a big deal. I promise."

Marisol sighs. "Okay, you're probably right. This could help you get some info."

I squeal. "Thank you! You are a genius for thinking to get that woman's card!"

"Well," says Marisol, a grin spreading across her face, "I know just how you can pay me back."

A sinking feeling spreads through my stomach. "No, please. I'll do anything but that."

Marisol's grin widens. "Sorry, Rachel Lee. Looks like this is the start of your modeling career."

Chapter 9

After I get home, I call Evan to tell him about Marisol's ideas for the Bake-Off.

"It sounds great," he says.

"And here's the best part. I think you should do the music."

Evan goes quiet.

"Hello?" I say finally. "Are you still there?"

"Yeah, sorry. It's just that I'm not in a band, remember? Not yet, anyway. And I don't think I'm brave enough to go up on stage by myself."

"Well, you have a month to get a band together," I tell him. "And even if you can't, think of it this way: if Marisol can force me to get up in front of everyone and *model aprons*, then you playing by yourself will be nothing."

He laughs. "Since when did you get so bossy?"

"Since you started encouraging me to talk. If you'd let me be my shy, mute self, you wouldn't have this problem."

I can practically hear him grinning over the phone. "Oh well. I guess I deserve what I get then, huh?"

"That's right."

"I wanted to ask you, what are you doing on Wednesday night? I was thinking we could go get some ice cream or something."

"Yes, please! Anything to get me away from here."

"Why, what's going on?"

"My mom's having a real-estate agent come over to see how much our house is worth."

Evan lets out a surprised half-cough. "Wait, what? You guys are moving?"

"No!" I cry. "It's just in case things don't pick up with the cleaning business."

"Wow. I thought the business was doing okay, even with the Ladybug people moving in." I hear him suck in a breath. "If you had to move, you'd still stay in town, right?"

"I–I don't know." I focus on a loose thread on my bed-spread, not sure what else to say.

"Well," he says finally. "We don't have to worry about that yet. Maybe not at all, right?"

"Right." Hopefully not ever.

● ● ●

The Prank List

That night, Mom lugs a big box into my room that she's labeled "Rachel's Things" in her scratchy handwriting.

"What's that?" I ask.

"Some items from the attic," she says. "It's high time we organized up there. Could you go through and see if there's anything you'd like to keep?"

I stare at her. Mom's been avoiding doing the attic for years. She's always said that it would be wrong to clean out the memories up there. And now here she is, emptying the place like it's a trash can.

I have a feeling this is connected to the real-estate agent's upcoming visit, but there's no way I'm going to ask Mom about that.

"Rachel?" she says. "I could really use your help."

I sigh. "Fine. I'll look through it."

She gives me a tight smile and hurries out of the room.

I get to my feet and pull up one of the flaps. The box is full of old toys and books and drawings. I unpack some beat-up alphabet books and laugh at the sight of Mr. Hip, a pink hippo that I used to sleep with every night when I was little. He's more gray than pink now, but he's still as huggable as ever. How could I have ever put him in a box?

I give Mr. Hip an apologetic kiss and place him on my

bed before I keep going through the box, surprised at how much easier this is than I expected. Then I grab a piece of paper that's sticking out of an old sketchbook and my stomach curls into a ball. On the crinkled paper is a crayon drawing I did when I was in kindergarten. It's of Mom and Dad and me and my imaginary turtle, Norm, all standing in front of my house.

Blinking furiously, I shove the drawing back in the box and slap the flap closed.

Chapter 10

When I get over to Marisol's house in the morning, I hear giggling coming from next door as I go up the walkway. I glance over and, as usual, Angela Bareli is perched on her porch swing spying on everyone who goes by. But for once Briana Riley is sitting next to her, giggling right along with her. It doesn't take a genius to figure out they're laughing at me, especially since they're both staring me down as I get closer.

"Good morning, Rachel!" Angela calls out. Then both of them start cracking up again.

My cheeks ignite. I try to ignore them, but I can't help freezing in my tracks as Briana says: "So I hear you're a thief now."

"What?"

"That's what my mom told me," says Angela. "She heard from our new cleaning lady that your old clients have been firing you guys now that you've started stealing jewelry."

"I didn't steal anything. I swear!"

"Like you swore you didn't make up a fake boyfriend?" Briana chimes in.

It's been weeks since anyone's brought up the fake boyfriend Marisol and I made up months ago to try to make Steve Mueller jealous. It was a giant mistake, and I swore I'd never do anything that dumb again. But I guess making up one huge lie makes people think I can't be trusted. Leave it to Briana to totally take advantage of that.

Briana fingers something at her throat, and I see she's wearing the other half of the necklace that matches Caitlin's. Maybe this is more about her hurt feelings than about me, I realize. If she still wears her necklace, then some part of her must miss being friends with Caitlin. The fact that Caitlin left her necklace behind without a second thought must have stung Briana's pride.

"I didn't take anything," I say. "The necklace must have just fallen somewhere."

Briana and Angela exchange knowing smiles. "Sure, Rachel," says Angela. "If you say so."

I want to knock their heads together like two melons.

To them this is all a game, a way to get back at me for encouraging Caitlin to leave them behind and start her own popular crowd. They have no idea how desperately my mom and I need the cleaning money.

The front door of Marisol's house swings open, and she comes outside with an uncertain look on her face.

"What's going on?" she says.

"Oh, we're just chatting," Angela answers. "Aren't we, Briana?"

Briana shrugs and looks down at her perfectly manicured nails. It's weird to see Angela suddenly taking the lead. For years, Briana has been the queen bee of my grade, doing whatever she wants and making everyone else miserable. But now that both her boyfriend and her best friend have dumped her, leaving her with the biggest social climber in school as her only friend, maybe she's a little less sure of herself.

Still, I don't exactly feel bad for Briana. She's been picking on me nonstop for the past year. She might be Evan's twin sister, but she is absolutely nothing like him.

When I go inside Marisol's house, her eyebrows are raised expectantly. "What was that all about?"

I explain what Angela and Briana said about people firing us because they think I've been stealing.

"That's crazy," says Marisol. "You guys have only lost a couple of clients, and for all you know, that's a coincidence."

"But how would they know the necklace is gone unless Ms. Montelle told someone about it? What if she never called my mom back because she hired the Ladybugs instead, and she told them about the necklace? If they start spreading that around town, we'll lose all of our business!" I take a deep breath. "Do you still have that Ladybug business card?"

Marisol nods and pulls the card out of her panda-shaped purse.

My stomach flutters at the thought of calling a total stranger, but I have no choice. "Okay, I'll ask how much they charge. Then I'll try to work in something about stealing to see if she brings up the necklace thing. And then I'll hang up. It'll be easy, right?"

Marisol looks a little skeptical, but she nods. I go lock myself in Marisol's bathroom—I definitely can't talk on the phone with someone listening!—and then dial before I chicken out. It rings a few times, and finally a woman's voice answers.

"Hello, is this Lillian?" I say, trying to lower my voice to sound older. Instead, it comes out weird and squeaky.

"Yes?"

"Oh, hello. My, um, my daughter, um, gave me your card. I wanted to ask about your…um, your price."

"My price?"

"No!" I cry. "Not *your* price, obviously. I mean, you're not for sale or anything! Um, no, just how much it costs to have you clean my house."

"Ah," she says, like she's finally figured out this isn't some kind of prank phone call. "I just need some general info." She starts asking me about the location of the house, the square footage, and the number of bathrooms. I do my best to answer her questions without saying anything else ridiculous. When she tells me how much the Ladybugs would charge, I realize it's pretty much what my mom would ask for, too. "We've recently expanded into your area," Lillian continues, "but the company has been in business for over five years."

That explains why I'd never seen the Ladybugs around town before a couple weeks ago. If they've been in business for five years, they've had plenty of time to get things down to a science. No wonder their employees remind me of cleaning machines.

"Hello? Are you still there?" Lillian says.

I realize she stopped talking a minute ago, and I've just been breathing into the phone. Maybe I *should* be a prank caller. I seem to be perfect for the job.

"Sorry. One more question," I say. My hand is so sweaty that the phone is about to slip out of it at any second. "Have you had any problems with, um, people, um, thieving things?" Oh my goldfish. *Thieving*? Who even says that?

"Not at all," she says. "In fact, we pride ourselves on being professional, unlike some other businesses in the area." She lowers her voice. "I don't want to gossip, but I've heard another cleaning service in town, one that's brand new, already has a pretty questionable reputation. That's not something you'd ever have to worry about with us."

"Do...do you know the name of the cleaning service?" I whisper.

"Lee Cleaners," she answers. "I'd watch out for them."

"Thanks," I mumble and hurry to end the conversation. When I hang up the phone, I feel sick. I open the bathroom door to find Marisol sitting on her bed with an expectant look on her face.

"What did she say?" says Marisol. "What happened?"

"It's not our prices. It's me. I'm the reason people are firing us."

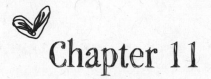

Chapter 11

After dinner, Mom rushes around the kitchen, scrubbing every surface she can find. It takes me a minute to notice that something's off. Then I realize what it is: Mom isn't whistling. Ever since she started dating Mr. Hammond, she's always humming or whistling or even—to my poor ears—singing. But today she has a far-off look on her face.

"Are you okay?" I ask her.

Mom glances up from scraping a saucepan and gives me an obviously forced smile. "I'm great," she says.

I can't help wondering if this is about us losing clients. I consider telling Mom what the Ladybug woman said about us, but I can't make myself do it. Not only will it kill her mood even more, but I already feel guilty enough that this is my fault.

I wish there was something I could do to prove to people that I didn't take that necklace, but what?

Then it hits me. What if I go over and help Ms. Montelle look for it? If we find it, then Lee Cleaners will have its reputation back. It might not convince our old clients to rehire us, but at least it'll keep us from losing any new ones.

If I call Ms. Montelle, I'm afraid she'll make some excuse and hang up on me. She's always been so nice, but ever since the necklace incident, I'm not sure how she feels about me. My best bet is to show up on her doorstep and hope she doesn't turn me away.

After telling my mom that I'm going to meet Marisol, I ride my bike over to Ms. Montelle's house. When she opens the door, I can tell she's just gotten home from work. Her business suit is rumpled, and she looks exhausted.

"Rachel," she says, almost sighing my name. "What a surprise. What are you doing here?"

"I wanted to come help you look for Caitlin's necklace," I say. "I feel really bad that it's missing. Even though I didn't take it. I promise."

She gives me a tired smile. "I guess it couldn't hurt to take another look."

We go into Caitlin's room, and I start peering into every nook and cranny I can think of. As Ms. Montelle helps me move the dresser and roll up the rug, I can't help wondering if she's watching me extra carefully to make sure I don't take anything else.

After a half hour, we still don't find anything. I'm so frustrated that I want to start throwing things, but I don't think that will exactly improve my reputation.

"We did our best," she says finally. "I suppose it's just one of those mysteries." Ms. Montelle smiles at me again, and I'm at least glad to know that she doesn't blame me.

As I leave her house, I notice that there aren't the usual piles of papers and dirty coffee mugs in the living room that my mom and I have had to clean up every weekend. Even though we haven't been to this house in almost two weeks. That's weird.

Then, on my way through the kitchen, I spot it: a Ladybug Cleaners magnet hanging on the fridge.

My feet freeze, like they're suddenly bolted to the floor. "Ms. Montelle?" I find myself saying. "Have you heard people saying bad things about my mom's cleaning business?"

She looks surprised. "I–I don't think so. Why?"

"Well, that new cleaning business, Ladybug Cleaners? I keep hearing rumors about them, so I wondered if people talked about us like that, too." Whoa, what am I saying? It's like my mouth is just going without me.

Ms. Montelle frowns. "What kinds of rumors have you heard about them?"

I wait for my mouth to make something up, but it seems to be done talking. "Um, only that they're not very good at their jobs, that's all," I say. "You might want to watch out for them." I realize I'm echoing what Lillian at Ladybug Cleaners said to me.

Ms. Montelle nods, her face still serious. "Thanks, Rachel. I'll keep that in mind."

As I pedal home, my mind is spinning faster than my tires. Part of me can't believe I just lied like that, but another part of me feels strangely hopeful. Maybe we *can* do something to fight back.

Okay, it might be low and sleazy to make up rumors about people, but isn't it pretty much the same thing the Ladybugs are doing to us? They have no proof that we're thieves, and yet they're telling everyone that to help their business.

They're the ones who started the fight. I'm flinging a little mud back at them, that's all.

Chapter 12

The next day, Mr. Hammond comes over to cook a surprise dinner for my mom. It was pretty bizarro when he called me a few days ago to plan the whole thing behind her back—I'm definitely not used to talking to my former vice principal on the phone!—but I know Mom will be surprised and happy.

"Thanks for helping me out," Mr. Hammond says as I work on making a salad while he pops some herb-crusted salmon into the oven.

"Sure," I say. We work in silence for a long moment. I feel a little awkward being alone with Mr. Hammond, but not nearly as uncomfortable as I'd be with anyone else who was dating my mom.

"So how's that pastry class going?" he asks finally.

I have to stop myself from groaning. "Okay, I guess. It's not really what I was expecting."

"If nothing else, it'll be good experience."

I smile weakly, hoping he's right.

"I have to admit something," Mr. Hammond adds. He clears his throat. "Tonight's dinner isn't just a surprise. I, uh, I wanted to ask your mom something."

I drop a hunk of lettuce on the counter. "Oh my goldfish!" I shriek. "Are you going to ask her to marry you?"

Mr. Hammond blinks at me. Then he chuckles. "Your mom is a wonderful lady, but we've only been out a few times. I'm not sure we're quite there yet."

"Oh." A rush of relief washes over me. Mr. Hammond is a nice guy, but my mom isn't even divorced yet. Plus, with my dad maybe coming back... But there's no point in thinking about that, I remind myself. I only have to worry about it when my dad is actually on my doorstep.

"I was going to ask your mom if she'd like for us to be exclusive. We haven't talked about it, but I don't think she's seeing anyone else. And I'm certainly not interested in dating anybody but her."

I almost laugh. Of course my *mom* is having an easier time with her dating life than I am. She's not even divorced yet and she has someone clamoring to be her boyfriend.

"But I wanted to make sure you were all right with

the idea before I talked to her about it," Mr. Hammond goes on.

"Me?" I'm flattered he would even care enough to ask. "I mean…I can't pretend it's not kind of weird, but she's happy, so that's good enough for me."

He smiles. "Great," he says, like the topic is over. But I can't help blurting out one last thing that's on my mind.

"Just please don't leave my mom like my dad did, okay?" I say. "She was such a mess after it happened. I don't think she could handle it again."

Mr. Hammond looks surprised. Then he smiles. "Don't you worry, Rachel. I'm not going anywhere."

And even though it's hard for me to believe him because my dad has been such a flake my whole life, I feel better.

* * *

After I finish helping Mr. Hammond make dinner, I head off to Marisol's house to give him and my mom some privacy. I definitely don't want to accidentally see any k-i-s-s-i-n-g!

When I get to Marisol's, we heat up some leftovers for dinner and then hang out in the living room watching silly reality shows. I have an hour before I'm supposed to meet Evan for ice cream, so if I'm going to fess up to Marisol, it has to be now.

"Okay, I have something to tell you," I finally say, knowing she's not going to like it. "I think I have a plan for how to get back at the Ladybugs for spreading those rumors about us."

"Yeah?" Marisol pops some broccoli into her mouth.

"After what happened last year with Steve and Briana, I swore I'd be honest with you," I say, "which is why I'm telling you this. But I know you'll think it's totally horrible."

She puts her fork down and gives me a steady look, clearly preparing for bad news.

I explain what happened at Ms. Montelle's house. "I didn't mean to lie to her, but it just happened. And afterward I was thinking, what if I don't stop there? What if I find a way to let more people know that there's something off about the Ladybugs?" I look for a reaction, but Marisol keeps staring at me with that same calm look.

"I know you think it's totally unethical," I go on, "but if Mom and I can't find a way to stop losing clients, then we might have to sell the house. My mom even has a real-estate agent coming over tonight, and she's started cleaning out the attic. I'm willing to try anything if it'll help!"

I wait for the explosion that I know is coming, but Marisol only nods, picks up her fork, and starts eating again.

"Aren't you going to say anything?" I cry. "This totally goes against all your die-hard rules."

She sighs. "I know it does, and if I had any better ideas of what to do, then I'd try to talk you out of it. But to be honest, if this will help your family, then I can live with it."

I stare at her for a second. Then I fling my arms around her. "Thank you," I whisper. I didn't realize how much I was afraid of her judging me. I guess it's time to come totally clean. "Hopefully this is a one-time thing, but just in case, I've started a list of other pranks I could pull on the Ladybugs."

Marisol frowns. "What kind of list?"

Reluctantly, I pull a piece of purple notepaper out of my pocket and hand it over to her. There are only a couple things on it so far:

Number 1: Start rumor about the Ladybugs.

Number 2: Replace their cleaning supplies with paint.

"Okay," she says. "So how are you going to start a rumor about them? You can't just say something is off about them again. People won't buy it."

She's right. Who knows if Ms. Montelle even took what I said seriously? "I know. I have to make up something really bad. And—this is going to sound crazy—I was thinking of telling the rumor to Mrs. Bareli."

Marisol gives me a blank stare. "Angela's mom?" Then she laughs. "Oh, good thinking. Between her and Angela, it'll be around town in less than a day. Do you think she'll believe you?"

"I don't know," I admit. "But what else can I do? I can't exactly fix it so the Ladybugs are caught doing something wrong."

Marisol and I look at each other. I can practically hear bells going off in both of our heads.

"Or maybe I can," I say. "But when? And how?"

"Well," she says slowly. "I know the Ladybugs clean Angela's house on Mondays, but as for how…I don't know."

We scratch our heads for a few minutes but can't come up with anything good. Finally, we give up and decide to think more about it tomorrow. It feels weird to have Marisol helping me plot something sleazy. I can tell she hates every minute of it, but I guess that's how much she cares about helping me.

I only hope this doesn't turn into another Fake Boyfriend Troy fiasco. I'm still not sure how I convinced Marisol to agree to that one, but I wish I'd listened to her when she tried to warn me that it was a terrible idea.

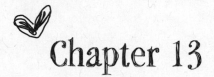

Chapter 13

When Evan and I go to Moo Pies for ice cream that night, I spot a group of kids from school on the other side of the parking lot. They aren't looking my way, but I can't help feeling giddy about the fact that they could glance over at any second and see that I'm here with a cute boy on a *date*. All those years of feeling like a total loser almost don't matter anymore, not when Evan Riley wants to be here with me!

After we order our cups of ice cream (mint chocolate chip for him and Moose Tracks for me), we go sit on a bench. Nearby are a couple of plastic cows that I guess are supposed to make the ice-cream stand look more authentic, even though I know for a fact they don't make their own ice cream.

As I sit there spooning bites of deliciousness into my mouth, I study Evan's adorable profile and try not to die from happiness. Everything else in my life might be confusing, but Evan is pretty darn wonderific.

"Have you found anyone to be in a band with you yet?" I finally ask.

"I've talked to a few people, but nothing definite."

"But you'll be ready in time, right? Because I kind of already told Marisol you'd do it."

He laughs. "I guess I don't have a choice, then, do I?" He shovels the last bite of ice cream into his mouth and crumples the paper cup into a ball.

For a second, I'm afraid he might be mad at how pushy I'm being about this whole thing, but he just drops the topic and asks: "So how are things going with the cleaning business?"

"Okay, I guess." I hesitate, wondering how much to tell him about my gossip-spreading plan. I definitely trust Evan, and I don't think he'd tell anyone about what I'm going to do, but I don't want him to think I'm a horrible person. We had enough of that when he caught me snooping around Briana's room a few weeks ago. Granted, he finally forgave me for that, and I promised that I'd be honest with him from then on. So I guess I have no choice but to tell him the truth like I did with Marisol.

After I explain the situation, he focuses on his spoon for a long minute. "So if this plan of yours works, there's a good chance you won't have to move?"

"That's what I'm hoping." I hold my breath, waiting for him to tell me how disappointed he is in me for planning to lie to people.

Instead, he smiles and says, "If I can do anything to help, let me know."

"Really?" I'm so relieved that I put my ice cream down, throw my arms around him, and give him a long hug. Then I realize what I'm doing and start to pull away, but Evan holds on to me.

Evan Riley is hugging me. In public. On purpose!

When he finally pulls away, he keeps holding my hand. Holy chopped parsley. Evan Riley is holding my hand!

"So listen," he says.

But at that moment I spot someone over his shoulder, and my stomach lurches. "Oh no," I say.

"What's wrong?"

"You know that guy from my pastry class I was telling you about? He's here." I watch as Whit and a little kid who could be his brother get in line to buy their ice cream. I quickly pull Evan away so that Whit won't spot us.

"Why are we hiding?" says Evan as I drag him behind one of the plastic cows.

"I don't want him to see us." It's hard enough to have a normal conversation with Whit in pastry class. Seeing him out of context will make things ten times more awkward.

"What's the big deal? He's not going to start throwing things, is he?"

"Probably not," I admit. "But…" I realize that Evan wouldn't understand. He's never been an outcast. He's never had to deal with people laughing at him for doing and saying the wrong thing all the time. "I'd just rather not see him," I say finally.

Evan shrugs, and I can tell he's trying to be understanding. Maybe I'm overreacting about the whole Whit thing, but before I can apologize, Evan says: "Do you want me to ride back to your house with you?"

"Oh. Sure." I guess that means our date is over.

● ● ●

When Evan and I get to my house, I slam on the brakes at the sight of my mom standing outside with a balding man who's holding a clipboard. They're both staring up at the roof, and I can hear him asking questions about the last time the shingles were replaced.

Oh no. This must be the real-estate agent. I was hoping he'd be gone by the time I got back.

Evan stops his bike next to me. "Are you okay?" he asks.

"No," I whisper, wondering if maybe I can ride off before my mom spots me.

"Rachel!" Mom calls from the driveway. "Come meet Mr. Colby!"

Too late.

I hop off my bike and turn to Evan, not sure what to say. Ever since we left Moo Pies, he's been weirdly quiet.

"Thanks for the ice cream," I say. "And for getting me out of the house with all that going on." I nod over my shoulder to where I can hear Mom rattling off the names of all the different bushes she's planted in the front yard.

"Anytime," Evan says, flashing a grin. "Whenever you need a break from evil real-estate people, just say the word."

My stomach relaxes. Maybe things between us are okay after all. I'm probably stressing over nothing. I glance over to make sure my mom isn't watching, and then I lean in and give Evan a quick, one-armed hug.

"Thank you," I whisper in his ear. Then, with my face burning at about a million degrees, I hurry away.

As I walk my bike into the driveway, Mom introduces

me to Mr. Colby and lists all the great things he's been saying about the house. I smile and nod, pretending to listen, but all I can do is replay the feeling of Evan's arms around me. As we go back inside, with Mr. Colby commenting on how well-maintained our brick walkway is, I don't think my feet touch the ground even once.

Chapter 14

Marisol and I spend most of the day on Thursday planning for the Bake-Off. For someone who practically prides herself on not having a lot of friends, Marisol was able to get a surprising number of people to sign up. We have volunteers doing sets and lights for the fashion show, and even a few people in charge of hair and makeup.

Marisol has already started sewing adorable aprons for everyone to wear in the show.

"Cherie and I were talking yesterday," Marisol chatters on, "and she said that if people like the aprons, Chef Ryan might even start selling them in his bakery. Can you believe it?"

"Wow, that's great!"

"I never thought aprons would be my thing, but fashion is fashion, right? And if even one person besides me wants to wear my designs, I'd say that's a pretty big win."

"Are you kidding? Pretty soon, Aprons by Marisol will be a chain of stores all over the world."

She giggles. "Yup, right next to Rachel's Pastries."

"We'll see about that," I say, rolling my eyes. "First I have to get through this pastry class."

"Watch. When you win the Bake-Off, Chef Ryan will see he's been totally wrong about you."

"*If* I win. They won't even let us prepare for the Bake-Off beforehand."

"I think that seems fair," Marisol says with a shrug. "Then everyone starts off the same, you know?"

"But what if they have us make something I've never baked before? What if I don't even make it through the semi-final round on the last day of class? What if—"

"Rachel, relax! You'll figure it out. You always do, right?"

A couple weeks ago, I would have said yes. Before I started the pastry class, I thought I could handle any baking challenge that came my way. Now I'm not so sure.

"Okay," Marisol says, holding up a purple apron with a lion face on it. "How about you try modeling this for me?"

"What?" I've been hoping Marisol will change her mind about this modeling thing, but so far she's been pretty determined.

"You better start practicing now so you'll be ready to strut down that catwalk on the day of the Bake-Off."

I groan and pull the apron on. It's not hemmed yet so it goes almost all the way down to the floor. Once I have it tied, I shuffle across Marisol's room.

"What are you doing, your best caveman impression?" she says.

"I'm walking!"

"I've seen you walk. What you were doing was lumbering. Look, try it this way." She demonstrates a runway walk that would make any supermodel jealous.

I feel ridiculous, but I try to mimic her, reminding myself that Marisol's stuffed animals won't judge me if I look like an idiot.

"That's better," she says. "At least you look like you're used to walking on two legs now. We'll keep practicing."

I rush to take off the apron in case she means more practicing right now. "So I've been thinking about the prank on the Ladybugs," I say. "My mom was looking at apartment listings yesterday, so I need to do something fast. If the Ladybugs are coming on Monday, then maybe I can sneak into Angela's house and leave something there to make them look bad. A clump of hair in the sink might do it."

Marisol thinks this over. "I know for a fact that Angela's going to be at the beach with Briana all day on Monday because she wouldn't stop talking about it when I saw her yesterday. But her mom might be home. How would you sneak in?"

"I could say I left something in Angela's room and go get it."

Marisol gives me a skeptical look. "She'd never believe that. Her mom knows you guys aren't friends. If it was me, she might not care."

My face must light up like a Christmas tree because Marisol all of a sudden starts backpedaling. "I'm not saying that *I* should be the one to do it," she says. "I couldn't lie like that to Mrs. Bareli's face!"

"You wouldn't have to lie," I tell her. "You could go over to Angela's house tomorrow and accidentally on purpose leave something in her room. Then on Monday, you could go get it."

She shakes her head. "That's still sneaky. And besides... I let Angela borrow a sewing kit a few weeks ago, so I wouldn't have to make anything up."

"Perfect!" I say, but I can see how much the whole idea pains her. It makes me feel like a jerk for even asking. "Sorry. If you really don't want to do it, then I won't make you."

I must look desperate because Marisol finally throws her hands up and says, "Okay, fine. I told you I'd do whatever it takes to help, so I will. But this is it, okay? If this doesn't work, I'm out."

"Thank you," I say, hoping she knows how much I mean it. The fact that she's willing to bend her morals of steel to help me is amazing. I don't mention that I've been adding more ideas to the Prank List (put mud in their shoes, post bad reviews online, and so on), mostly because a lot of them are silly, but also because I doubt Marisol wants to hear about them.

I figure the Prank List is like a hand grenade. I hope I never have to use it, but in battle, sometimes you have to do awful things to protect the people you love.

● ● ●

Normally, Mom and I spend Thursday evenings cleaning houses, including Mr. Hammond's. But this week, Mom announces that we're changing our schedule.

"We'll do our Thursday clients on weekends, now that we have more flexibility." She doesn't say that the "flexibility" is because we keep losing people every week. "Plus," she adds, "cleaning Robert's house seems a little silly now."

"Why?" I say, grinning. "Because he's your official new boyfriend?"

Mom blushes and doesn't say anything. I guess that means the whole thing embarrasses her. But hey, if she can drag me into conversations about my crushes, then I can make her talk about hers.

"You never told me how your special dinner went," I say.

"It was very nice." I expect her to go on, but she doesn't. Before I can press, she says something about having to go organize her receipts and heads off to her bedroom.

Maybe that means the dinner with Mr. Hammond didn't go as well as he was hoping. Or maybe she feels weird about having a boyfriend when she's still technically married. If the guy was anyone but Mr. Hammond, I'd feel weird about the idea, too.

A second later, Mom pops her head out of her bedroom and asks, "By the way, have you finished looking through that box of things from the attic?"

I gulp. Since that first night, I've been pretending the box doesn't exist. Like there's a big square of invisibleness in the corner of my room.

"Um, almost," I say.

"Try to do it soon," she says. "I'd really like to get the attic cleared out."

I promise her that I will, but I don't think either of us believes me.

Chapter 15

I get to pastry class early on Saturday, ready to show Chef Ryan what I can do. I'm so early that he's still setting things up, but when I ask if I can help, he waves me away.

I spot Mr. Leroy in the corner, poring over the directions for today's assignment. He's bent over the paper, squinting through his bottle-thick glasses and obviously still having trouble reading the list of ingredients.

"Do you need some help with that?" I finally ask. I haven't had a lot of experience with old people—Dad's parents live on the West Coast and Mom's both died before I was born—so anyone with all-gray hair usually scares me, but Mr. Leroy looks pretty desperate. Plus, he's about half my height, so if he tries to suck the youth out of my bones, I should be able to defend myself.

He straightens up and gives me a denture-ific grin.

The Prank List

"That would be lovely," he says. "I think Ms. Gomez is getting pretty tired of reading things for me."

I assume Ms. Gomez is the woman with the kindergarten-teacher smile. I can't imagine her getting tired of helping anyone.

As I go over the ingredients, Mr. Leroy nods his head slowly like he's trying to memorize them. Then he lets out a dry laugh. "Seventy-six years old and I'm only now learning how to cook. Can you believe it?"

"Better late than never, right?" I say, sounding like my mom.

"My wife was always the cook in the family. I tried to help her, but she didn't like how I accidentally set things on fire." He laughs again and pushes up his enormous glasses. Then his smile fades. "Now that she's passed on, it's just me."

I swallow. This is exactly what scares me about old people. Not only do they have a hard time hearing me since I'm quiet and shy, but half their stories end with someone dying. How are you supposed to respond to that?

"I'm sorry," I manage to choke out, hoping he doesn't start crying or something. Then *I'll* probably start bawling, too.

Luckily, he smiles again and says, "Well, I figure if I'm going to learn, it might as well be now." He glances over as Chef Ryan stomps out of the room. "I only wish our teacher was a little more patient," he adds in a whisper.

"No kidding!" I say. "At least he doesn't hate you. He can't even stand to look at me."

Mr. Leroy chuckles. "I don't think the young man hates you. He's just a grump, that's all. Like my old cat, Martha. She gets cranky when things aren't done her way."

The thought of Chef Ryan as a cranky old cat makes me smile. I can imagine him hissing at anyone who gets too close to his favorite cutting board.

"Aha!" says Mr. Leroy, like he's caught me red-handed. "I knew there was a smile in there somewhere."

That makes me smile wider. Maybe old folks aren't that scary after all.

Other people have started filing into the kitchen, and Chef Ryan storms past with a bunch of ingredients. As I head over to grab an apron, Whit comes in. He's wearing his leather jacket yet again, which is plain nutso in the July heat.

"Hey," he says, coming over to me. "Want to team up?"

I'm shocked he'd want to work with me again after seeing my "inferior" chocolate chip cookies. But since everyone else seems to have already found a partner, I guess I don't have a choice but to agree.

As we get our ingredients together for today's project—maple-glazed éclairs—Whit doesn't say a word, so I find myself blabbing on about how Marisol has been talking to Cherie on the phone practically every day, making plans for the Bake-Off.

"It's going to be huge," I tell him.

Whit's face goes from bored-looking to a little green. "I didn't think there'd be a ton of people there besides our class. At my school, the crowd was always pretty small."

Wow, who knew Mr. Confident could be as freaked out by the idea of getting up in front of a bunch of people as I am? "I was hoping it would be kind of small, too, but I think it'll be good for the bakery, you know? Plus, that way the winner will feel really official."

Whit nods. "It *will* be nice to win in front of everyone."

I snort. "So you just assume you're going to win?" Just when I start thinking Whit might not be such a bad guy, he has to go and say something like that.

"Why? You think you can beat me?" His eyebrows shoot up.

"Yes! I won a big competition at my school this year,

with a cash prize and everything. I know I can win this, too." I'm not usually the type of person to brag, but come on. How can Whit assume he's going to win? Even I'm not that full of myself when it comes to baking.

He shrugs. "I guess we'll see."

I could scream at the smug look on his face, but at that moment I see a Ladybug van zip past the bakery window.

"Ugh!" I cry. "I can't believe it. Those things are stalking me!"

"What things?" he says.

"Those vans." I point just as the minivan turns onto another street. "They're trying to put my mom's cleaning company out of business."

"What are you talking about?" For once he looks mildly interested in what I'm saying, but I'm not about to start spilling my secrets.

"Never mind." I go to grab the recipe, but Whit's already swiped it.

"Step one," he reads in that loud, slow voice of his, like he's talking to a toddler. I can't stand to listen to it for another second. Anything is better than that.

"You want to know about those vans?" I say, cutting him off. "Why they're ruining my life?"

The Prank List

He looks up from the recipe, clearly interested again. "Why?"

"If you make the filling and let me make the dough—without micromanaging me—I'll tell you," I say.

Whit thinks this over for a second and then nods. As we get to work, I tell him about my mom's business losing clients because of the Ladybugs and about my plan to plant evidence at Angela's house to get back at them. It takes me forever to explain, mostly because I keep having to stop to do another part of the dough recipe. Beside me, Whit just listens and works on the filling without even looking at the instructions.

"It's fighting fire with fire, you know?" I say as I start squeezing lines of the dough mixture onto a baking sheet. "I don't like the idea of doing it, but hopefully it'll even things out again so that we won't lose any more clients."

Whit nods slowly as he works on the maple glaze now that the crème filling is done. "What if they make up another lie about you guys?"

I drop a whisk so that it goes clattering into the sink.

"Rachel!" Chef Ryan calls across the room. "Be careful!"

"You think they'd really do that?" I ask.

Whit shrugs. "I don't know. What if they come up with an even bigger lie to tell? What will you do then?"

I hadn't thought of that. Foolishly, I'd imagined my one lie would be the end of it. But if telling a few more is what it takes, I guess I'll have no choice. "I'll do what I have to."

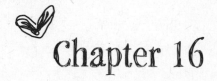

Chapter 16

When Mom asks me about class during dinner that night, I mumble something and focus on shoving food in my mouth. I was convinced that our éclairs had come out great, but Chef Ryan only pursed his lips after he tried one and said we should spend less time talking and more time following instructions. Every time I think about it, I want to strangle something.

After dinner, I'm still in a terrible mood, so I'm relieved when Evan calls to invite me over to watch reruns of *Pastry Wars* with him.

As I ring the doorbell, I'm hoping his sister doesn't open the door. So, of course, I see her unsmiling face when the door swings open.

"Oh," she says. "It's you."

"Hey, Briana," I say. "Um, is—"

She doesn't even wait for me to ask if Evan is home.

Instead, she turns on her heel and stomps down the hallway. At least she leaves the door open instead of slamming it in my face. In Briana terms, that's practically a warm welcome.

"Hello?" I call, poking my head inside. "Evan?"

"Rachel?" I hear him call back. "I'm in the living room."

It feels strange to walk around his house as a guest and not as a cleaning lady. Even though we could use the money, I'm glad Mom decided we shouldn't clean the Rileys' house anymore. It would be super weird to be scrubbing a toilet with my maybe-sort-of-kind-of-boyfriend in the next room. I bet that's why Mom stopped cleaning Mr. Hammond's house.

When we curl up on the couch to watch the show, Evan surprises me by putting his arm around me. A shiver goes through my whole body. Evan Riley has his arm around me!

I snuggle into him, enjoying the peppermint-and-soap smell of him. I've never felt so happy.

"How was your class?" he asks during a commercial.

I sigh. "Fine, I guess. I'm pretty sure Chef Ryan hates me. At this rate, he'll never let me be in the Bake-Off."

"What about Whit?" Evan asks. "Will he be in it?"

"Probably, at least if you listen to him. He thinks he's

the best pastry chef in the world and that he'll win the Bake-Off with his eyes closed. Isn't that obnoxious?"

I expect Evan to agree with me, but he's frowning at the TV, which is weird since there's still a commercial on. Then again, I guess I have been whining about my class a lot.

"Sorry to complain so much," I add. "It's just that the class isn't what I thought it was going to be."

Evan nods. "I understand. It's okay." But his voice sounds strange.

I wish I could ask him what's wrong, but I'm afraid what his answer might be. Even though he's sitting here with his arm around me, he might be starting to wonder if he's made a huge mistake. Maybe that's why he hasn't asked me to be his girlfriend yet.

When the show is almost over, Briana marches through the living room on her way to the kitchen. She shoots us a disgusted look.

"Get a room," she mutters. As she walks away, her phone beeps. She glances down at it and then puts it in her pocket. A minute later, it beeps again. Briana ignores it as she digs around in the fridge.

Almost immediately, I hear her phone start to ring.

Evan shakes his head in amusement. "Angela's been stalking her all day," he says.

"Angela Bareli?" I ask stupidly, as if it could be anyone else.

"Yeah, I think Briana's getting pretty sick of her, but Angela can't take the hint. She keeps calling and texting and—"

Ding dong!

"And coming over," he finishes as the doorbell echoes through the house.

I turn to Evan, my mouth open. "Do you think that's her?"

He nods. "She's always 'in the neighborhood' whenever my sister doesn't answer her calls."

"Creepy," I say as the doorbell rings again.

"Briana!" Evan calls into the kitchen. "Are you going to let your stalker in?"

Briana rushes back through the living room. "Tell her I'm not here," she says before darting up the stairs.

Evan chuckles and waves for me to follow him. Whatever weirdness was between us seems to be gone. I guess I have Angela to thank for that.

When Evan opens the door, sure enough, Angela Bareli is standing on the stoop grinning back at us.

"Hi, Evan!" she chirps. Then her eyes go over to me

and her smile dims a little. "Hi, Rachel." I have to give her credit for at least pretending not to hate me. "Is Briana home?"

"Um, no," says Evan. "She's out. I can tell her you stopped by."

"Could I wait here until she gets home?" she says.

Evan blinks, clearly surprised by the request. "Um, I don't think that's a good idea. She'll probably be gone a while."

Angela's face falls. "Oh. Okay. Well, I'll try back later." She smiles her totally fake smile and hurries away.

As we watch her prance down the street, Evan turns to me. "You don't think she's going to lock my sister in a basement and try to take over her identity, do you?" he says.

"Hmm, just in case, you might want to tell Briana not to go anywhere by herself." I sigh as my mom's car pulls into the driveway. "Time to go."

Evan reaches out and takes my hand in his. Then he squeezes my fingers and waves as I walk away.

My hand doesn't stop tingling for what feels like hours.

Chapter 17

On Monday morning, Marisol and I watch as Angela hops into Mrs. Riley's car all decked out for the beach. She can barely fit in the backseat, thanks to a sun hat that's easily the size of a satellite dish.

My body is pumping with nervous energy when the Ladybugs pull into the Barelis' driveway a few minutes later to clean the house. I can tell Marisol is even more nervous than I am. I try to distract her by asking her to tell me about the wacky personalities Andrew has been dealing with at film camp, but her eyes keep going to the window any time a car drives by.

Finally, after the Ladybugs leave, it's showtime.

As we make our way out of Marisol's room, I notice her hands are shaking.

"It'll be fine," I say as we leave her house. "Angela's mom won't suspect anything."

The Prank List

Marisol nods and goes toward the Barelis' front door, while I rush around the side of the house and ease my way through some bushes. Then I stand under Angela's bedroom window, trying not to look too conspicuous.

A minute later, I hear the doorbell ring and then catch snippets of Marisol explaining to Mrs. Bareli how she let Angela borrow a sewing kit a few weeks ago and how she's wondering if she can come in and look for it since there's a special needle that she needs for a project she's working on.

I hold my breath as Mrs. Bareli lets Marisol in. The minute the door closes, I count a few seconds to give them time to go upstairs. Then I pull out my phone and dial the Barelis' number.

"Hello?" Mrs. Bareli says after a few rings. Yes! That means Marisol is currently all alone in Angela's room, free to plant an enormous hairball in the middle of the carpet. Now I have to give her some time.

"Yes, hello," I say, trying to make my voice sound older and more official. "I'm calling about your latest order with…" My mind goes blank. I open my mouth and close it again. Nothing.

"My order from where?" she asks.

"Uh…penguins!" I call out, blurting the first word that comes to mind. Oh my goldfish. Did I really just say that?

"Penguins?" she repeats. "Is this some sort of joke?"

"No! No, ma'am. Of course you didn't order penguins. That would be ridiculous. Where would we even get penguins this time of year?" I clear my throat, stalling. "I'm calling from, um, Penguin Refrigeration about your latest freezer purchase."

Great. She'll tell me she didn't order a freezer and hang up on me.

"Did my husband call you? We've been talking about getting a deep freezer for years, but as far I know, we didn't… Wait!" She lets out a laugh. "I see now. This must be a surprise for my birthday. It's coming up in a few weeks. I probably shouldn't even be talking to you!" She giggles in a way that reminds me of Angela.

Uh-oh. I'd wanted to distract her for a little while, not get her hopes up about a birthday present that will never come.

"Is there a problem with the order?" she says.

"Oh, um…no, we're just confirming it."

Suddenly, I hear Marisol in the background. "I found the needle," she calls. "Thanks, Mrs. Bareli!"

That's my cue to hang up. I try to think of something to say to Mrs. Bareli to help smooth things over, but my mind is unhelpfully blank again. Finally, I wish Mrs. Bareli a happy birthday and hang up. Then I run like the wind to the back door of Marisol's house, almost tripping over a garden hose on the way.

A minute later, while I'm still panting, Marisol opens the door for me and lets me into the house. She's grinning like a monkey, which I guess means her part of the plan went smoothly.

When we go up to her room, we both erupt in hysterical giggles.

"I can't believe that worked!" says Marisol. "Did she suspect anything on the phone?"

"I don't think so," I say. "Although next time you see Mr. Bareli, you might want to convince him to buy a freezer."

Marisol's smile fades, and she looks at me with a strange expression that almost looks like guilt. "So, I didn't totally follow the plan."

"What do you mean?"

"When I got to Angela's room, I went to put the hairball in the middle of the carpet, but then I saw her favorite T-shirt on her chair. You know, the one she got from Disney that she wears all the time? And I thought, the Ladybugs are accusing you of stealing. Why not make people think that they steal things, too? So I..." She lets out a nervous laugh. "I took it."

"You *stole* it?"

"No! I only moved it. I put it under her bed where she probably won't find it for a while. So I didn't steal it. It's still in her room. But she'll think the Ladybugs took it."

My head starts pounding. Tricking Angela feels wrong, but at the same time, Marisol might be right. Maybe the prank needed to be bigger to really get people's attention.

When I tell Marisol that, she grins. "I can't believe it, but I actually had fun! I felt like James Bond or something."

I shake my head. Clearly, I've unleashed Marisol's dark side. I only hope I can stuff it back into whatever dungeon it came from before it does any actual damage.

● ● ●

After dinner that night, I watch Mom slumped at the kitchen table, sifting through a mountain of bills. I can see the frown lines on her face from all the way across the room.

"I don't understand," she says. "We were finally doing

okay a few weeks ago." She sounds tired and defeated, which is totally bizarro coming from her, Ms. Optimism.

"We've only been cleaning houses for a few months," I say. "Maybe we need more time."

She sighs. "I wish I knew why we're losing so many clients. I've been trying to spread the word around town, but it doesn't seem to be doing any good. I think there's too much competition."

I consider telling Mom about the rumors about us, but I can't imagine how much more defeated she'll look. Besides, there's nothing she can do about the rumors. And if she found out that I was playing dirty, too, she'd flip out.

"Would you mind asking some of your friends if they could mention our service to their parents?" she says.

"Um, Mom?" I'm about to remind her that I don't have friends. Then I shut my mouth, partly because I have more friends now than I've ever had before, but also because I want her to see that I'm on her side. "Sure. I'll spread the word."

It hits me that maybe there are different ways of advertising that we haven't tried yet. It's not enough to stop losing business. We need to find ways to get new clients, too.

Maybe something as simple as putting up flyers around town would help.

I'm willing to try anything if it means never having to see my mom look so defeated again.

Chapter 18

When I go over to Marisol's house the next morning, I'm actually looking forward to seeing Angela Bareli sitting on her front porch. Maybe I'll get some hint about whether or not our plan worked.

But, for once, Angela isn't there. The porch swing just sways back and forth like there's a ghost sitting on it. I wonder if that means Angela's off stalking Briana somewhere.

When I knock on Marisol's door, she doesn't greet me with her usual smile. Instead, she's furiously chewing on her lip.

"What's wrong?" I say.

She shakes her head and waves me up to her room. I barely have time to smile at her mom, who's hunched at the dining room table with her laptop, before Marisol grabs my elbow and drags me up the stairs.

"I heard Angela freaking out last night," Marisol says

after she's closed her bedroom door behind us. "She was yelling so loud I could hear it all the way up here."

"Was it about the T-shirt?"

"I think so," says Marisol. "She was yelling something about it being her favorite one, and she seemed really mad at her mom."

Uh-oh. "Do you think she blames her mom for taking her T-shirt and not the Ladybugs?"

"I don't know, but it doesn't look good."

We sit in silence for a second. Did our plan totally backfire? As far as I can tell, Mrs. Bareli is a pretty nice person. I'd feel awful if she had to deal with even more of Angela's diva-ness because of us.

"I can't believe this," says Marisol, putting her head in her hands. "Why did I have to take her shirt? Why couldn't I stick to the plan?"

"Because you were trying to help me," I say softly. "Because you're the best friend in the universe."

She looks up at me. "I just hope I didn't make things worse."

"No way," I say. "Let's wait a few days and see what happens. If Angela still thinks her mom took her shirt, we'll find some way to get her to look under her bed. It'll be fine."

Marisol nods. It's funny that for once I'm the one comforting her and not the other way around. It makes me wonder if I haven't been that great of a friend recently.

"Want to work on the mural?" I say. "That always makes you feel better."

She smiles. "Okay, as long as we can go over the Bake-Off stuff again."

I nod and hand her some chalk so she can do more outlines on the wall. Then I turn on a couple of window fans and start filling in a tiny section of sky with bright blue paint.

"So where are we with the planning?" I ask.

"Everything's all ready to go except for the music, but you said Evan could do that, right?"

"I'll ask him about it this afternoon. We're supposed to go hang up flyers before dinner."

Marisol grins at me, looking like her regular self again. "You guys are the cutest couple."

I feel myself blush. "We're still not official, so I don't know if you can call us a couple."

"Yes, I can. Hanging up flyers is pretty serious business. It's practically a wedding ceremony."

"If that's true, then you and Andrew are heading toward flyer-hanging at any second. You're perfect for each other."

Now it's her turn to blush. "I feel like I haven't seen him in forever. I wish the summer would go by faster!"

I can tell she really misses him. Emails and stuff are fine, but it's not the same as actually getting to see your boyfriend all summer.

"He'll be back before you know it," I say. "When is he getting home?"

"The day before the Bake-Off," she says. "I guess that's not too far away." She sighs and steps back to admire her newest sketch, which includes a shop that looks a lot like Ryan's Bakery. "When does Chef Ryan pick the finalists?"

"The last day of class. We'll have a mini Bake-Off that morning, and then three people will go on to the finale the next day."

"And you'll be one of them, of course," says Marisol. "Even if Chef Ryan is a weirdo, he can't deny your stuff is awesome."

"We'll see. I have three weeks to get my technique perfect. But honestly, as long as I beat Whit, that's all I care about."

"You really hate that guy, huh?"

"He's so full of himself! You should see his leather jacket. He wears it all the time, even when it's a million degrees outside. He totally thinks he's better than everyone else, and he's convinced he's going to win the Bake-Off."

Marisol smiles. "Maybe we should fix him up with Angela. They sound perfect for each other."

"Oh my goldfish. I think the universe would implode if those two got together." I sigh. "I guess he's not that bad, but I definitely don't want him to win."

"Don't worry. You'll bake his socks off."

I laugh. "That sounds gross. I'm totally imagining a pie full of dirty socks."

"Ew!" Marisol sticks her tongue out in disgust. "I don't think you'll win the competition with stinky sock pie!"

We start giggling and joking around as we keep working on the mural, and we don't stop until we hear someone yelling outside. We hurry over to the window to see Angela standing out in the driveway, right in front of a Ladybug van. Next to the van is Lillian, the owner of Ladybug Cleaners.

Marisol and I exchange looks and then quietly turn off the fan and open the window so we can eavesdrop.

"What did you do to my shirt?" Angela is yelling. "It's my favorite one and now it's gone!"

I can't hear what Lillian says back, but she's shaking her

head and looking confused. Suddenly, I feel sorry for her, especially when Angela marches up to her and starts yelling about how she's going to get her mom to fire the Ladybugs.

"Angela!" Mrs. Bareli says, coming out of the house. "I'll handle this." Then she sends Angela inside while she has a quiet conversation with Lillian. Whatever happens, I don't think Mrs. Bareli fires her since they wind up smiling and nodding at each other before Lillian hops back in her van and drives away.

Guilt shoots through me like an electric shock. I feel bad that Lillian got yelled at for something she totally didn't do.

But she deserves it, I remind myself. The Ladybugs have been spreading lies about us for weeks. Because of them, my mom and I are closer to losing our house than ever before. Sinking to the Ladybugs' level might make me feel like dirt, but it's the only way out of this mess.

Chapter 19

T hank you for coming with me," I say for the tenth
time as Evan and I lock up our bikes in the center
of town. For some reason, going to hang up flyers on my
own feels too scary, though I'm not sure what I'm afraid
of. Paper cuts?

"No problem," he says. Then he grabs the flyers in one
hand and gently takes my hand in the other. I almost faint
as his fingers interlock with mine.

We go to the library, the town hall, and a bunch of other
places, taping and stapling the flyers to every surface we can
find. Marisol helped me make up the flyers this morning,
and I think they came out pretty cute—even though they
have a picture of me holding a mop on them.

When we pop into a few of the stores, including the
consignment shop that Marisol loves, Evan is mercifully
willing to do the talking. I can just imagine me trying

to ask if we can hang up flyers and finding some bizarre way to offend people. Or to promise them freezers for their birthdays.

Finally, the flyers are all gone and I'm feeling better. These will have to get us some new business, right? Marisol and I added a few more ideas to the Prank List today, but I really don't want to use them. The whole Angela T-shirt incident was bad enough.

"Want to go get some lunch?" Evan asks, pointing to a sandwich shop down the street.

My stomach rumbles in response, which makes him laugh.

"Okay, I'll race you!" he says. Then he flashes a devilish grin and takes off.

"Hey!" I yell. "Cheater!"

I glance down at my skirt and my flip-flops, which are meant more for lounging by the pool than running. But I don't want Evan thinking I'm a wimpy girl. So I take a deep breath and break into a sprint.

There's no way I can catch up to Evan, but I'm going to at least put in a good effort. I'm so busy keeping an eye on how far ahead he is that I'm not paying attention to where I'm going.

Suddenly, one of my flip-flops catches on something—a

rock?—and I fly forward. I scramble to catch myself before I crash into the sidewalk, but it's no use.

I belly flop onto the ground and lay there for a minute, feeling totally dazed and wondering why the breeze feels so...breezy all of a sudden.

When I finally start to move, my stunned brain vaguely registers that my skirt is all the way up to my waist.

Wait. *What?*

"Ahh!" I shriek, snapping out of my daze. Oh holy pickled pineapple. My underwear is on display for everyone in town! I ignore the ache in my arms and scramble to pull my skirt down as Evan comes running toward me.

"Are you okay?" he says, catching his breath.

I nod, still sitting on the ground, my face burning. Did he see my underwear? Did I cover it in time? Wiping out in front of him is bad enough. He does *not* need a peek at my cupcake-print undies.

"You're bleeding," he says, gently touching my chin.

"I'm okay," I say, trying to stand up. Evan helps me get to my feet, still looking concerned. My knees are a little skinned, but mostly I'm mortified.

"I'm sorry. I shouldn't have taken off like that."

"Really. It's not a big deal." As long as you didn't see my underwear, I add silently.

Evan walks me over to a bench and has me sit down for a while to make sure I'm totally okay. It's sweet how worried he is about me, but it also makes me super self-conscious.

"So listen…" he says right as I blurt out, "So how's the band search going?"

"What?" we both say at the same time. Then we laugh in unison.

He motions toward me. "You first."

"I was just asking how the band search was going," I say.

Evan stiffens. "Okay, I guess. I talked to some people from my school. We're supposed to meet this weekend to go over a few songs."

"That's great!" I say. "You guys will rock."

He shrugs like he's embarrassed. Then his face lights up. "I forgot to tell you. Briana said Angela is really unhappy with Ladybug Cleaners. I'd say that means you'll be getting more business any day now."

"Oh. Good," I say meekly, remembering Lillian's stunned face as Angela screamed at her. I hate myself for not telling Evan the whole truth about my Ladybug smear campaign, but admitting what Marisol and I did feels too icky, especially when he's being so sweet. I'll tell him about it later, I decide.

"So, what were you going to say before?" I ask.

He opens his mouth and closes it again. Then he shrugs. "I forgot."

"Brain fart!" I say, giggling, which makes Evan laugh, too. I get to my feet, careful to keep my skirt firmly in place. "Now, how about that lunch?"

Chapter 20

When I get home from Marisol's house the next day, I'm surprised to see my mom sitting at the kitchen table, staring down at a piece of paper.

"I thought you and Mr. Hammond had a dinner date right after work today," I say.

She doesn't even look up.

"Mom? Are you okay?"

Finally, she glances at me, her brow furrowed. "Why would someone do this?" She holds up the paper, and I realize it's one of the flyers Evan and I put up yesterday. When I get closer, I see why my mom is so upset.

On the picture of me with the mop, someone's drawn devil horns and a mustache. As if that wasn't bad enough, at the bottom of the flyer, underneath "Lee Cleaners," someone's scrawled "SUX" in thick, angry letters.

I stare and stare at that awful, misspelled word.

"Every flyer I saw today during my lunch break had this on it," Mom says. "I don't understand why someone would go to all that trouble to play a joke like this."

I sink down next to her and put my hand on her shoulder, trying to be comforting, but inside I'm shaking with fury. If one flyer was vandalized, that could just be some random kids having fun. But this is bigger. Whoever did this knew it would hurt us.

"And the worst thing is," Mom says softly, "one of our clients called today and said she's been hearing unflattering things about us, and that she prefers to go with a company that's more established." She shakes her head. "I don't know what we're doing wrong."

I can't believe it. The rumors about us are only getting worse!

My anger starts to bubble over, and I jump up and rush to preheat the oven. Baking is the only thing that might make me feel better right now.

I gather ingredients, slamming drawers and cabinets so loudly that my mom gives me a pained look.

"Sorry," I mumble.

"What are you making?" she asks.

"I don't know yet."

She sighs. "Well, I hope it's something good. I could use a little cheering up."

As I work on what I realize are going to be lemon squares—Mom's favorite—I keep thinking about someone defacing all of those flyers. It must have been the Ladybugs. Who else would take all that time to mess up each one? They know we're competition and they're lashing out. I guess Whit was right. One jab at the Ladybugs isn't enough to bring them down.

I need to hit them again.

As I shove the lemon squares into the oven, I'm still shaking. But this time it isn't with anger. It's with determination.

Forget small battles. This is all-out war.

When the lemon squares are cooling, Mr. Hammond calls the house looking for Mom, but she asks me to tell him that she's not feeling well and that she'll call him back later. Then she goes off to her room without even trying a lemon square.

I don't have much of an appetite, either. Instead, I go to my room and take out the Prank List, looking for something that I can do tonight. My eyes stop on "post bad online reviews." That would be pretty easy. And it's nice and public, just like the flyers the Ladybugs destroyed.

The Prank List

It takes me more than an hour to find every listing for Ladybug Cleaners that I can online. Their reviews are all glowing, at least in the areas where they've been cleaning houses for the past five years. There aren't any reviews for our town yet, but that's about to change.

I start making up different fake names and submitting all kinds of bad reviews, from the "they stole my hairbrush" type to the "they purposely threw away my great-aunt's cremated ashes" kind.

I know I should feel bad about what I'm doing, but I don't, not when I hear the low hum of Mom's TV through the bedroom wall and imagine her in bed, curled up in a ball, maybe even crying. I feel like a lioness whose cub has been messed with. Anyone who hurts my family is going to get their head clawed off.

Finally, when I'm done with my smear campaign, I search for reviews of Mom's business out of curiosity. I'm surprised that we actually have one. Someone gave Lee Cleaners an outstanding review and said nothing but nice things about us. I suspect it might have been Ms. Montelle, although I guess she doesn't feel that way about us anymore. Hopefully, all my efforts will give us a chance to change her mind.

● ● ●

The next night, I can barely pay attention when I'm on the phone with Evan. I'm still so riled up about the whole flyer thing.

"Are you okay?" he asks after a couple minutes of me barely grunting answers at him.

"Sorry, I guess I'm distracted."

"It'll be okay," he says. "You'll find some other way to get more clients." It's like he can read my mind without me even having to tell him why I'm so preoccupied. Then again, I guess I'm not all that hard to read.

"Thanks," I say. "I hope you're right."

"Hey, I was thinking of having some friends over on Saturday night to watch *Pastry Wars*. Most of them have never seen it before. Do you want to come? You can finally meet everyone."

I swallow. The idea of meeting Evan's friends is both exciting and terrifying. What if they hate me?

"It'll be fun and really low-key," he adds. "I promise."

I guess I'll have to meet them eventually. Maybe it's best to just get it over with. "Okay. I'll be there."

"Great. I was thinking of stopping by the bakery and picking up some stuff for the party. Maybe I'll come during your class so I can see you in action."

"No!" The idea of Evan watching me messing everything up and getting yelled at by Chef Ryan is mortifying.

"Why not?" he says.

I feel silly telling him that I'm embarrassed, so I say the only thing that comes to mind. "There's no point in you buying stuff for the party when I can bake something and bring it over."

"Oh." He sounds disappointed. Did he really have his heart set on visiting my pastry class? "Yeah, I guess that's okay. I'll see you on Saturday?"

"I'll be there," I say. Then before I can say anything else, he hangs up the phone.

Chapter 21

Right before class starts on Saturday, I remember that Marisol insisted I measure all the students for the fashion show. I sigh and reluctantly pull her hot-pink measuring tape out of my bag.

"Um, Whit?" I say, deciding to get the worst over with first. "Can I, um, measure you?"

He looks surprised for a second. Then he grins. "You want to see how big my muscles are, don't you?" He flexes his arms like a bodybuilder. It makes me want to smack him.

"It's for the fashion show! My friend is making aprons for everyone. Cherie told us about it, remember?"

He chuckles, clearly loving seeing me all flustered. I grit my teeth and tell him to get into the position Marisol showed me. Then I measure him as fast as possible as he keeps grinning the whole time, like I'm secretly enjoying every second of it. Yeah, right.

I write down the measurements and then quickly go through the other people in the class, trying not to die from embarrassment at having to touch them.

Finally, I get to Mr. Leroy. When I explain what I need, he shakes his head. "Oh, I don't think I'll be going to the Bake-Off."

"What? But you have to! Everyone else is going. We'll have music and stuff. It'll be fun."

"I'm sure it will," he says. "But it's the anniversary of my wife's passing. I think I'll spend the day thinking about her, instead."

I suck in a breath. "Oh." Suddenly, I feel terrible. Of course he wouldn't want to spend the day doing something like that when he still misses his wife like crazy.

"It's all right," he says, patting my hand. "You kids have fun. I'm sure you'll win the whole thing." He gives me a big wink.

"Thanks," I say.

As I go back over to my table, I groan inwardly as I see that Whit's set up shop next to me. Even though we get to work alone today, I bet he'll still be criticizing everything I do.

When class starts, I'm looking over the recipe for today's

chocolate-dipped cannolis when Whit leans over and says, "So how did your plan to thwart the Ladybugs go?"

I shrug like it's none of his business and start measuring out ingredients. Who even uses words like "thwart," anyway?

"Okay, fine," Whit says after a minute. "I promise not to look over your shoulder while we're making the cannolis if you tell me what happened. Deal?" I don't know why Whit is so interested in this whole saga—maybe it's better than listening to my nonsensical nervous babbling—but I'm willing to milk it for all it's worth.

"Deal," I say. As we get our materials ready, I tell him about how we succeeded at planting evidence in Angela's room and how the Ladybugs got back at us with the flyers. I don't mention "stealing" Angela's shirt since that feels more like Marisol's secret than mine.

As I talk, my voice shakes with anger. I've never seen my mom so sad for so long, not even after my dad left. I keep expecting her to go back to psychotically organizing things like she does when she's stressed out, but ever since the flyer incident, mostly she's been moping around the house and sighing a lot.

"How do you know it was someone from the other cleaning business who messed up the flyers?" Whit says.

"Who else would go to all that trouble?"

He shrugs. "I guess that's true. So what are you going to do?"

"Well, I already did one thing the other night." I tell him about the bad reviews I posted.

"Doesn't that seem kind of extreme?"

"No! We haven't gotten a single response to our flyers, not one! After I spent all that time making them and hanging them up everywhere. Not only are the Ladybugs taking our business away, but they're keeping us from finding any new clients. I'm just returning the favor."

"Rachel!" Chef Ryan calls across the kitchen. "Less talking. More cooking!"

My cheeks go instantly hot. I don't think I've ever been scolded for talking too much. At school, my teachers are always telling me to talk more.

I focus on filling my cannolis while Whit starts dipping his in chocolate.

"Well, if you think of another way to get back at them and you need some help," he says after a minute, "let me know."

"Wow, thanks," I say softly. Maybe Whit isn't that bad of a guy after all.

He steps back and looks at one of his finished pastries. "This looks pretty darn good, if I do say so myself."

Scratch that. He's still as full of himself as ever.

"By the way," he says, "I was at Moo Pies with one of my nephews last week. I thought I saw you there."

My cheeks go hot again. "Um, yeah, I was there. I guess I didn't see you."

"Was that guy you were with your boyfriend?"

I stare down at my cannolis. "I–I don't know. We haven't exactly talked about that, um, yet." Why am I telling Whit this? It isn't any of his business. Why does he even care, anyway?

"Oh," says Whit. "Well, I hope—"

Before he can finish, Chef Ryan calls out that our time is up. He has us line up like we're in the army so he can inspect our cannolis. Mine look a little lopsided, but I think they taste okay. Hopefully, Chef Ryan will finally see that I'm not a total failure.

Mr. Leroy is first, and Chef Ryan lifts what looks like a charred lump off his shaking plate. I expect him to yell at Mr. Leroy the way he'd yell at me if those were my cannolis, but he only shakes his head and continues down the line.

The Prank List

Whit, of course, gets high praise from Chef Ryan. I can practically see his head swelling.

Then Chef Ryan stops in front of me and inspects my cannolis for a long time. "Let's hope they taste better than they look," he says finally.

He breaks off a corner and pops it in his mouth. Then he cringes and makes a big show of spitting the bite into a napkin.

I can't believe he just spit out my food!

"Rachel, did you not hear me say that you should drain any excess water out of the ricotta?"

I gulp. "Um, no. I heard you."

"But you didn't do it."

"Well, no. I—I was afraid it would make the filling too dry. The last time I made these at home, that happened, so I—"

"So you decided to ignore the instructions." Chef Ryan cocks his head to the side. "Tell me, Rachel. If you already know how to make everything, why are you taking this class?"

My mouth drops open. I don't even know what to say.

"You know what would happen if you were a professional chef and you ignored the instructions because you were stubborn and wanted to do things your own way?" he asks.

I shake my head.

"You'd get fired." He marches away, leaving me staring at the tile floor, desperately trying not to cry.

Chapter 22

When Mom picks me up after class, I'm still shaken by what Chef Ryan said. I can't believe he thinks I'm such a failure. Maybe I was kidding myself about becoming a pastry chef one day.

Usually, the minute I'm upset, Mom can sense it like she's got a mood-o-meter in her brain. But today, she's as grumpy as I am, probably because yet another one of our clients called this morning to "let us go." Every week, we have fewer houses to clean.

I shudder as I imagine the day when we have no clients at all.

"No." There is no way I'm going to let that happen.

"What?" Mom says, glancing over at me.

Oops. I hadn't realized I'd said it out loud.

"I just, um, hope business picks up again soon."

Mom sighs. "I wish we could do some more advertising,

but it's too expensive. And making more flyers seems like a waste of time."

"Do you think maybe Mr. Hammond would help?" I ask, realizing that might be a solution to at least some of our problems. Now that he and Mom are officially a couple, he'd probably be happy to pitch in.

Mom's lips pull into a tight line. "I can't ask him to do that."

"But he's your boyfriend now. Isn't that kind of what boyfriends do? Help you out if you need it?"

She shakes her head. "I will not allow Robert to solve my problems. I made that mistake once, and I will not do it again."

It takes me a second to realize what she means. "You're talking about Dad, aren't you?"

She sighs. I feel like more and more, she's been starting every sentence with a sigh. "Your father wasn't a mistake. I don't mean it that way. I only mean that I put my faith in someone who disappointed me. Both of us. I can't do that again. From now on, I'm going to depend only on myself."

"And on me, right?" I ask.

Mom actually smiles and reaches out to squeeze my hand. "And you. Honestly, Rachel, I don't know what I would have done all these months without you."

I wonder if this is why Mom hasn't been spending as much time with Mr. Hammond recently. Maybe she wants to prove to him, and to herself, that she can do things on her own.

As we pull up to our first house of the day, I keep thinking about what Dad said about maybe coming back home. What if he asks me about it again? Or if he finally brings it up with Mom? How will he react when he finds out that she is never really going to let him back into our lives?

● ● ●

When I get home, the last thing I feel like doing is baking, but I promised Evan that I'd make something for the party, so I try to quiet Chef Ryan's voice in my head and get to work.

But he won't shut up. I can hear him criticizing every move I make. I try to slam cupboards and pans around to drown him out, but Chef Ryan just talks louder in my head. Great. I'm totally losing my mind.

"What are you making?" Mom finally asks from the living room. "Percussion pie?" She laughs weakly at her terrible joke, but I can hear the strain in her voice.

"Butterscotch macadamia cookies," I say.

"Can you try making the quiet version?"

Maybe it's a good thing I'm leaving the house later. Having the two of us under one roof can't be safe. We might set the place on fire with our extreme crabbiness.

I'm barely paying attention as I grab the rest of the ingredients. I want these cookies to be done so I can stop hearing Chef Ryan saying, "You'd be fired," over and over again.

As I go to grab the baking soda, my phone rings. It's Dad.

I can't deal with talking to him right now, not when he might tell me that he was only kidding about moving back up here, and not when he might ask me about my class and accidentally make me burst into tears over what happened today. So I let it ring and ring as I scoop some baking soda out of the box and dump it into the batter.

"Are you going to answer that?" Mom asks after the fifth ring.

"My hands are dirty," I say, which is only sort of a lie.

I shove the phone farther down the counter with my elbow and breathe a sigh of relief when it finally falls silent. Then I slide the cookies into the oven, slam the oven door closed, and go to get ready for my "date" at Evan's house.

Chapter 23

When I ring Evan's doorbell, I'm shaking all the way to my toes. Even the plate of cookies in my hands is wobbling. I was too scared to try the cookies after I made them, thanks to Chef Ryan's voice in my head.

Right as I'm about to dump the cookies in a nearby bush and make a run for it, Evan opens the door.

"Hey," he says, his face lighting up at the sight of me. "We were just going to start watching."

He steps in to hug me, but I kind of duck out of the way and shove the plate of cookies into his hands instead. I'm still so upset that I can't deal with anyone touching me. There's too high of a chance I'll burst into tears.

Evan frowns but doesn't say anything. Instead, he walks me down the hallway into the living room.

"Hey, everybody," he says to the three guys sitting on the couch. "This is Rachel." He goes down the line and does introductions, but I forget everyone's names almost the second I hear them. The first guy is tall and stick-figure skinny, the second has the biggest and blondest afro I've ever seen, and the third is small and toadlike in a way that's actually kind of cute.

"Hi!" I whisper, trying to wave but only managing to smack the side of my own head. Classy.

"Rachel made cookies," says Evan. He unwraps them and makes a big deal about how good they look. I get fixated on my shoes and don't look up as the guys crowd around the cookies and dig in. Normally I love watching people enjoy my baked goods, but not today.

And then the coughing starts.

First Blond Afro starts making weird phlegmy sounds. Then Stick Figure grabs his soda and chugs it like he's trying to wash down the cookie before it kills him. And finally, Toady spits part of the cookie back into a napkin, making me flash back to Chef Ryan spitting out my cannolis in front of everyone.

"Are they that bad?" I whisper.

Evan's the only one who hasn't taken a bite yet. He picks up a cookie and takes a nibble.

"They taste like..." He's obviously having a hard time swallowing. "Like..."

"Soap," Blond Afro chimes in. The others nod.

I stare at them. Soap? How is that possible? And then I remember my phone ringing while I was making cookies, me angrily dumping white powder into the batter, barely paying attention to what I was doing. Is it possible that somehow I'd used dishwasher detergent instead of baking soda? As crazy as that sounds, the two boxes were right next to each other on the counter. And I was really distracted.

Oh my goldfish.

"I'm so sorry!" I cry.

Evan laughs like it's no big deal. "You can't poison us that easily, Rachel Lee!"

I can tell he's trying to make me feel better, but it doesn't work. I can feel my face burning. I've been in Evan's house for all of three minutes, and already I've practically killed his friends. Luckily, they all look fine now—I don't think any of them got more than a bite—but I still feel horrible.

I can't believe this. Is Chef Ryan right? Should I just quit? I used to think I was a great pastry chef, but in the past few weeks I've done nothing but mess up in one major way after another. And now I've started almost poisoning people!

"Okay, let's watch some *Pastry Wars*," Evan announces.

But I'm already making my exit. "I can't. Sorry. I have to go."

"What? But you just got here."

"I know," I say as I push past him into the hallway. "I'm sorry."

Evan doesn't give up that easily. He stops me before I get to the front door and says in a low voice, "Don't worry about the cookies. Trust me, it's not a big deal. Those guys will eat anything."

"No, it's not just that."

"Then what?"

The way he looks at me makes me want to tell him about what happened in pastry class today, but I can't open my mouth. If I do, I'll start sobbing, and I can't do that, not in front of Evan, not when his best friends are in the next room.

"Sorry," I say before darting out of the house.

"Rachel!" I hear him call after me, but I don't turn back.

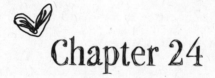

Chapter 24

The next night, Mom pokes her head into my room even though I don't feel like talking to anyone. She comes to sit on my bed and laughs at the sight of Mr. Hip propped up against my pillow.

"I forgot about this little guy," she says, stroking his faded pink ears. "You used to go everywhere with him. Even into the bathtub."

"No wonder he's all lumpy," I say.

Mom sighs. "Rachel, I know you've been having a rough time, so the last thing I want to do is make things worse. But..." She clears her throat. "I was just talking to my sister, and I mentioned to her that I was thinking of selling the house and—"

I sit up. "Aunt Nelly?"

Mom nods. "And she offered to let us stay with her for a while so we can save some money."

"But she lives all the way in Connecticut!" Not to mention the fact that she hates anyone who's under the age of twenty. She always calls me "the child" like I don't even have a name.

"Nothing is decided," Mom says, "but I wanted to let you know that it was a possibility. The truth is, honey, that unless something changes, we're starting to run out of options."

My body sags as I think of having to leave not only our house but our town. Leaving Marisol, Evan, school, and even Ryan's Bakery.

Mom pulls me toward her and kisses the top of my head. "We'll figure it out," she says into my hair.

A second later, my phone starts ringing. It's Marisol.

"Do you want to answer that?" Mom says.

I shake my head, but she's already getting to her feet. "It's okay. We can talk later. I know you'll probably want to tell Marisol about this."

After my mom closes the door behind her, I brush away a stray tear and answer the phone.

"Rachel?" Marisol says. "Are you busy?" Her voice is low and serious in a way that instantly makes me nervous.

"Are you okay? Did something happen with Andrew?" I ask.

"No. It's nothing like that…" She lets out a long breath. "I probably shouldn't even be telling you this. I know you're still upset about the whole poison cookie thing, but I—"

"Tell me." The last thing I want to think about is what happened at Evan's yesterday. He hasn't called me, which should make me happy since I don't have to explain why I ran off, but it also makes me feel worse that he doesn't care enough to check up on me.

"Fine," she says. "But don't freak out, okay? You know how you posted those reviews of the Ladybugs? Well, I was just looking at them and—"

I gasp. "Did they take them down? They can't do that, can they?"

"No, they're still there. But while I was on there, I noticed some new reviews about…about you guys. Ones that weren't there before."

"Were they bad?" I say softly.

"Um, yeah… They're, um, kind of…"

"Marisol, spit it out! I thought you weren't afraid to be honest, right?"

She sighs. "Okay, you're right. I'll just tell you. They talked about the stealing, which I guess is kind of to be expected, but then they said a bunch of other things. Really bad things."

"About us?"

"About you."

I blink, trying to understand what she's getting at. Then I realize that she means the bad things are about me personally, not about our business in general. "Where are the reviews?"

"I don't think you should read them," she says. "I wanted you to know because—"

"Tell me. I need to see them."

Finally, after a lot of badgering, she tells me which websites they're on. When I look through the reviews, tears start stinging at my eyes. "Rachel is immature." "The owner's daughter is a klutz." "The girl is a reported thief." The words float in front of my eyes.

"Rachel, are you still there?" Marisol says after a minute.

I clear my throat, pushing back the tears. "Uh, yeah. I'm here."

"I'm sorry," she says. "If I'd known this would happen, I would have talked you out of putting up those reviews in the first place."

I laugh bitterly. "Are you kidding? I'm glad I did it. Doesn't this prove that the Ladybugs deserve it? The question is, what prank am I going to do next?"

"Do you think that's a good idea? Maybe you should—"

"I'm not giving up. Not when my mom just told me we might be moving to Connecticut if we can't find a way to turn things around here! I'll only give up when those stupid Ladybugs are gone from this town for good."

There's a long silence, and I start to wonder if Marisol's hung up the phone on me.

"You really might move to Connecticut?" she says.

"Yeah. To go live with my aunt. I can't let that happen, Marisol. You don't know what she's like."

There's another long silence. "Okay," she says in a soft voice. "I know I said I was done, but I'm not going to let you do this by yourself. If you need my help, I'm in."

I squeeze my eyes shut. "Thank you," I say. At least I'm not in this alone.

Chapter 25

Marisol and I spend hours the next day racking our brains for a plan to strike back at the Ladybugs, something that will ruin their reputation in town and get them to leave me and my mom alone for good.

We pore over the list of pranks, but none of them seems good enough.

"I don't know," Marisol says finally, flopping on her bed. "If we start slashing their tires so they can't get to their jobs, that could do the trick, but we might also get arrested."

I sigh. "Right. Note to self: Avoid getting arrested." Still, Marisol might be on the right track. If we can find a way to keep the Ladybugs from getting to work on time... "I know! We do something to their cars so they can't get to their jobs."

Marisol stares at me. "Isn't that exactly what I said?"

"You were talking about slashing tires. I'm talking

about something that won't go on our permanent record if we're caught."

"Like what?"

"Hmmm, do you think we could track down a few dozen ladybugs and let them loose in one of the vans?"

Marisol smiles. "Probably not, but I see what you mean. We just want to annoy them enough to throw off their day."

"Exactly. If a bunch of the Ladybugs can't get to work one day, I'm sure their customers won't be too happy about that." I scratch my head. "Now we have to figure out where they park their vans overnight."

"How do you know the vans are all at the same place?"

I explain about the first time I saw the vans while I was at my pastry class, a whole fleet of them going down the street like they'd all come out of the same spot. "It must be somewhere near the bakery."

"But they've been cleaning houses in other towns for years. Why would they park their vans there?"

I shrug. "Who knows? Maybe they needed more space or something. The important thing is that we pretty much know where they are."

"And now all we have to do is find them." Marisol

laughs. "I never thought being corrupted by you could be so much fun."

As she adds our ideas to the Prank List, looking as excited as she did the day she hid Angela's T-shirt, I have to tell myself I'm doing what I have to do. Just because I'm bringing my perpetually honest best friend over to the dark side doesn't mean I'm a bad person. It means I'm desperate. Once this is all over, Marisol will go back to her old self, and she'll never have to lie or cheat or do anything bad for me again.

● ● ●

After we've told her mom that we're going to the consignment shop, Marisol and I ride our bikes into town to search for the Ladybugs' home base. I'm imagining some kind of nest or hive in between buildings where the red-and-black vans hang out in webs. But chances are, it's something way more boring like a parking garage.

We get to Ryan's Bakery and lock up our bikes.

"Now what?" says Marisol.

I think for a second. "Well, the kitchen is in the back of the building, and I saw the vans going past the window heading from…" I try to orient myself, but a sense of direction has never been one of my gifts. "Maybe that way?"

Marisol shrugs and heads in the direction of my pointing finger. I follow, keeping an eye out for any flashes of red.

As we go past the bakery, I peer inside, dreading seeing Chef Ryan. I sigh in relief when I spot Cherie behind the counter instead.

"Is Chef Ryan really so bad?" Marisol asks, like she's read my mind. She does that way too often. I guess it's a sign of how well she knows me.

"He's..." I try to find the words to explain. "He keeps telling me every technique I've ever used is wrong. Wouldn't you freak out if someone looked at your clothes and told you that they were done the wrong way?"

Marisol thinks about that for a minute. "I'd be upset, sure. But then again, if it was some big fashion designer telling me that, I'd probably listen to his advice. I mean, he's the one doing it for a living, right? I'm only self-taught."

I tuck my hair behind my ears, trying to decide whether what Marisol said is wise or infuriating. "I guess," I finally say. "And I guess he does know a lot. I just wish he didn't make me feel so bad about every little thing I do wrong."

She gives me a sympathetic smile. "I know. And that

part stinks. But you know you're good, no matter what he says. Right?"

"Are you forgetting that I practically poisoned Evan's friends?"

She rolls her eyes. "That was an accident. You were distracted. It doesn't mean you're a bad chef. Evan knows that."

"I haven't talked to him since then. I think he's ignoring me."

"Are you kidding? Of course he's not ignoring you! You're the one who ran out of his house, remember? He probably thinks you're upset and he's giving you space or something. You need to be the one to make the first move."

"But what if—?"

"What if nothing," she says. "You and Evan are perfect for each other. Are you going to let things get weird between you two over some semi-poisoned baked goods?"

She's right, as usual. "Okay, I'll call him tonight. Anything to get you to stop bossing me around."

She makes a big show of sticking her tongue out at me. Then her eyes widen and she grabs my elbow. "Look," she whispers.

I turn to see a parking lot next to a big building that

used to be a toy shop but is now totally deserted. Half the spaces are empty, but the other half are filled with mini-vans. Red and black ones.

Bingo.

Chapter 26

After I call Evan and apologize profusely for running out of his house after the cookie incident, he agrees to come over the next afternoon while Mom is out with a friend from work. I've decided it's time to tell him about all the stuff that's been going on with the Ladybugs. I know he probably won't approve of the pranks I've been pulling (even if the Ladybugs totally deserve what they get), but I'm hoping he at least won't try to stop me from doing them.

But when I open the door for him, my resolve goes out the window. His green eyes twinkle back at me like he's genuinely glad to see me. How could I do anything to mess that up?

"Hey, Booger Crap," he says, flashing a crooked grin. "I'm glad you invited me over."

"Me too. I'm sorry again about the whole cookie fiasco. No one had to go to the hospital, right?"

He chuckles. "Nope. I just wish you'd gotten to hang out with the guys. I think they'd really like you."

I smile. I guess that means everything's forgiven.

When we go snuggle up on the couch, I'm in heaven. I wish I could erase all the other craziness in my life and stay in this moment forever.

"So how was class the other day?" Evan asks.

I stiffen, replaying the things Chef Ryan said to me. I don't want to repeat them to anyone, not even to Evan. "Okay, I guess. I…I'm not sure I'm meant to be a chef after all."

He stares at me. "What are you talking about? It's like your dream!"

"I know, but…well, you didn't see the other people in my class. Some of them are way better than me. Whit's cannolis were amazing, and mine…" I shake my head, blinking back tears.

When I glance over at Evan, I'm surprised to see an odd look on his face. Not sympathy but something else…disappointment?

"You worship that Whit guy, don't you?" he says in a tight voice.

"What?"

"You talk about him all the time and you're always saying how much you hate him, but I can't help wondering…"

I nearly choke. "Are you saying that I like Whit? Like, *like like* him? No way! That's crazy!"

Evan doesn't look convinced. "Admit it, Rachel. You do like him. That's why you made me hide when we were at the ice-cream place, so he wouldn't see you with me. And that's why you didn't want me to come by your pastry class. So if you're planning to dump me for him, go ahead and do it, okay? At least then I'll know where I stand."

"Dump you?" I whisper. "*Dump* you?" A sudden wave of rage crashes through me. "How could I dump you when we're not even official? I keep waiting for you to ask me to be your girlfriend, but you never do! I'm not the one who doesn't want to be with you. You're the one who doesn't want to be with me!"

Evan jumps to his feet, his cheeks suddenly red. "I *was* going to ask you to be my girlfriend. That's the whole reason I asked you out for ice cream in the first place. I was just about to do it when you spotted Whit and got all weird on me. After that, I didn't know if it was worth saying anything to you anymore. I didn't want to make a total fool of myself."

I stare at him. He was going to ask me to be his girlfriend?

He had it all planned and I ruined it by freaking out? Can that really be true?

"Well, aren't you going to say anything?" he asks. I've never heard him sound so mad.

The idea of me liking Whit is so ridiculous that when I open my mouth to deny it again, a loud snort-laugh comes out instead. How could Evan think I would ever choose someone like Whit over him?

But the minute the laugh echoes through the room, I know I've made a huge mistake. Evan's face goes almost purple, and he turns toward the door. "I should get going."

"No, wait! I didn't mean to—"

"Sorry, Rachel. I think we both need some time to think about stuff."

"What about… What about the Bake-Off? You'll still be there, right?" I could kick myself in the head. What's wrong with me? Evan is pretty much saying we need a break from each other, and I'm asking him about the stupid Bake-Off?

Evan looks at the floor. "I don't think so." Then he turns and walks out of my house.

● ● ●

When Mom comes home, I'm curled up on the couch with

Mr. Hip under my arm, staring at the blank TV screen like I've been doing ever since Evan stormed out.

"Rachel?" she says. "Is everything okay?"

It's weird that I haven't cried. Maybe I'm still in shock that he would break up with me. *Did* he break up with me? I have no idea. I still can't believe the argument we had. It's like a bad dream.

"Rachel?" Mom asks again.

"I…I'm…" I'm not fine. I can't even say the word because it's so untrue. "Evan left."

She sits down next to me. "Did you guys have a fight?" she says, her voice soft and gentle.

It wasn't a fight. It was something more, something worse. "I don't know. It might be over."

"Oh, honey," she says, putting her arm around me. "I'm sorry. I know how hard that is."

And she does know, I guess, but her sympathy doesn't make me feel any better. I just feel empty and drained, like someone opened a valve and most of me leaked out.

"Is there anything I can do to help?" she asks.

Rewind time? Keep Whit from ever showing up in my life? Make me into a different person, one who doesn't always do the wrong thing?

"No," I say. "I think I just need to mope for a while."

"I understand." She gives me another squeeze and then heads to the kitchen. "How about I make us some dinner?"

That snaps me out of my daze. Mom hasn't made dinner in years, not since I started cooking every chance I got.

"How about some lasagna?" she says. "Grandma's special recipe?"

I smile weakly. It's been forever since I've had the lasagna recipe that my grandma passed on to my mom, but I can't imagine anything more comforting. "That's perfect. Thanks, Mom."

As I sit there curled up on the couch, watching her bustle around the kitchen, the tears finally start trickling down my face and plopping onto Mr. Hip's fur. I'm afraid they might never stop.

Chapter 27

The next day, when I tell Marisol what happened between Evan and me, she coos at all the right places and is furious on my behalf.

But when I tell her the part about him accusing me of liking Whit, she goes weirdly quiet and starts twisting one of her rings around her finger.

"What?" I say. "*You* don't think I like Whit, do you? That's crazy!"

"I know," she says, "but you have been talking about him a lot. I can see how Evan would get the wrong idea."

Great. So I totally deserve Evan being mad at me. "Okay, but why would he pull out of the Bake-Off? Does he hate me so much that he doesn't even want to be around me anymore?"

Marisol's face goes pale. "Wait. He dropped out of the Bake-Off? Just him or the whole band?"

"I...I don't know."

"Because if we have no band, there won't be any music! I don't think I can find someone else in a week, and I don't even have any sound equipment for us to play music on. Evan was going to bring amps and stuff. The flyers all say 'live music' on them! What are we going to do?"

I hadn't even thought about how this might mess things up for the Bake-Off. "I'll talk to him," I assure her, even though it's the last thing I want to do. I can't leave Marisol high and dry like that. "Maybe I can convince him to do it."

"Thank you," she says. "And once he and his band are done playing, then we can smack him for being such an idiot."

I smile weakly. "Thanks."

"Okay," she says, clapping her hands. "Enough moping around. We need a revenge plan!"

At first I think she means revenge on Evan, and I start imagining all sorts of movie-style ways to make him regret ever letting me go—most of them involving glam makeovers—but then she grabs the list of possible Ladybug pranks.

"So we need to do something to the Ladybug vans," she says, "but all we have written down so far is 'Put ladybugs in vans.' I don't think we can go to the insect store and buy some."

"All right." I take a deep breath. "What else could we do?"

We start listing other possibilities: Laying out nails to puncture their tires. Toilet-papering the vans. Putting gunk on their windows.

At the last one, a lightbulb flickers on in my brain. "Gunk," I repeat.

"Gunk?" says Marisol.

I smile my best villain smile. "I think we might have to make those Ladybugs an extra special batch of caramel."

* * *

When Mom gets home from work that night, she looks even more miserable than she has the past few days.

"Did we lose another client?" I ask, trying not to count how many (or few) that leaves us.

She shakes her head. "Robert and I had a bit of a disagreement."

"About what?" I can't imagine Mr. Hammond fighting with anyone. He's like the jolliest person ever. He probably tutored Santa.

"Nothing, really. He was hoping we'd go out tonight, but I was too tired."

"Isn't that the third time in a row that you've canceled on him?" I ask.

Mom purses her lips. "You sound like him. But it's not some conspiracy. I have a lot going on."

I don't point out that Mom's also been avoiding his calls the past week. "Shouldn't hanging out with your boyfriend make you feel better?"

Mom just shakes her head and doesn't answer. I guess that means she doesn't want to talk about it. "How are you doing?" she asks me. "Are you hanging in there?"

I know she's asking about Evan, but I don't want to talk about that, either. I guess Mom and I are both in serious funks.

"I'm fine," I say.

She can clearly tell that I'm lying, but she doesn't pry. Instead, she says, "I think I need to go lie down for a while. Would you mind making dinner?"

I almost laugh at her question since I always volunteer to make dinner. Then again, I have to admit I haven't been enjoying cooking and baking nearly as much since I started taking the pastry class. Pretty ironic, huh?

"I'll wake you up when it's ready," I say.

Mom gives me a quick peck on the forehead. "Thank

you, Rachel. I don't know what I'd do without you." Then she goes to her room and closes the door.

Her words keep throbbing in my head as I start making dinner. What would she do without me? Well, for one, no one would be accusing her cleaning employees of stealing things. And she wouldn't be in the middle of an online review war. I wish I could at least tell her what's going on, but I can't, not when it would break her heart.

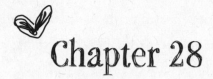

Chapter 28

When I show up at Evan's door after dinner, I'm expecting him to slam it in my face. It's been two days since our fight and my emotions are still sparking like live wires. I can only assume he's feeling the same way. But the Bake-Off is in a few days, and I promised Marisol that I'd help her if I could.

"Rachel," he says when he opens the door. "Hi."

"Hi." I stand there staring at him, wishing suddenly that I'd baked something so at least I'd know what to do with my hands. Except who knows what kind of poison I would have accidentally put in this time? "Um, can I talk to you for a second?"

"Sure."

I expect him to let me in, but instead he comes out of the house, shuts the door, and sits on the front steps. After a second, I sit next to him, careful not to get too close, which means I'm practically sitting in a prickly bush. Evan's trademark peppermint smell wafts toward me, and for once it makes me feel sick. How did things go totally wrong between us?

"How are you?" he asks stiffly, like we're strangers.

"Fine. I'm fine. Fine." Wow, if there was ever a way to show him how *not* fine I am, I definitely just did it. "Um, Marisol sent me over. Because of the Bake-Off. She really needs your band to play."

"Oh." He scratches his head, not looking at me. "I don't think I can do that."

"But you already have a group together! You guys are all ready to go. Can't you put the stuff between us aside for one day and help Marisol and Chef Ryan and everyone else out?"

"It's not because of you. It's..." He leans down and fiddles with one of his shoelaces. "I can't sing in front of people, okay? I can't do it."

"What? Why?"

"Call it stage fright or whatever, but I've always been terrified of performing. I agreed to do the show because I didn't want to let you down, but I can't do it. It's just not possible."

"Why didn't you tell me?"

Finally, he looks me in the eye. "I tried, but it was never the right time or you weren't really…"

He doesn't need to finish. I think of the way I totally messed up him asking me to be his girlfriend. Am I that bad at listening to people?

"Anyway, I'm sorry," he says. "I can't do it. To be honest, I never got a band together. I tried jamming with a couple of friends, but I couldn't even play in front of them. That's how bad it is."

"But the flyers all say there's going to be live music."

"Tell Marisol I'm sorry," he says again, getting to his feet.

"Wait!" I cry, jumping up to face him. "Isn't there anyone else who might be able to do it? Please, Evan. She doesn't even have sound equipment."

He thinks for a minute and then nods. "I'll see what I can do." Then he goes back into the house, leaving me alone on the steps.

As I'm about to drag myself home, the door opens and Briana storms out.

"Oh," she says, practically knocking into me. "What are you doing here?"

"I was just leaving."

I start to head down the walkway when Briana pipes up behind me. "It sucks when you get dumped, doesn't it?"

I turn around, expecting a cruel look on her face that says how much she's enjoying the fact that her brother finally realized I'm a loser. But her expression isn't snide or mocking. It's actually something like sympathetic.

"Yeah," I answer. "It's the worst."

Briana reaches up to run her fingers over the BFF necklace around her neck, and I realize she's not talking about getting dumped by Steve Mueller. After all, they only dated for a couple months. She's talking about Caitlin, her best friend for most of her life. Caitlin who now wants nothing to do with her.

I open my mouth to say something comforting or reassuring, something I never thought I'd do around Briana. But just then footsteps come up behind me.

"What are you doing here?" a voice says in a tone that I think Briana invented. Sure enough, Angela Bareli is standing on the walkway behind me, glaring at me like a dog that's afraid of someone taking away its food.

"Nothing," I say. Then I rush away from that house as fast as I can, leaving Briana with her new, horrible BFF. I never thought it was possible for me to feel bad for Briana.

And I don't, not exactly. But the truth is, I used to envy her. I used to think her life was perfect. Now I wouldn't trade places with her for anything.

Chapter 29

After my mom drops me off at Marisol's on Friday morning, we get right to work. Luckily, her mom is out meeting with a client, so we have the house to ourselves. Otherwise, it might be tricky to explain why we're making entire vats of caramel.

Finally, when we're done, we ooze the caramel into Tupperware containers and carefully stack the containers in our backpacks. Then we lug the bags over to our bikes. Pedaling into town is way harder with pounds of goo strapped to my back, but it'll all be worth it when we put those Ladybugs in their place.

We lock up our bikes behind Ryan's Bakery and then heave the caramel down the street. Hopefully, we don't look too suspicious.

Finally, we get to the parking lot where we saw the Ladybug vans the other day. There are nine parked here right now. Score.

The Prank List

"Ready?" I ask, suddenly nervous. Even if we probably won't get arrested for what we're about to do, we'll still get in huge trouble if anyone finds out.

"Let's do this," says Marisol, sounding not much braver than I feel. I squeeze her elbow, beyond grateful that she's here with me, especially since I know she'd rather be doing anything other than this sneaky stuff.

We glance around one more time to make sure no one is coming, and then we rush into the parking lot and pull out the first two containers of caramel. Luckily, the caramel hasn't had a lot of time to cool so it's still pretty gloppy. I pop the top off mine and stand over the windshield of a nearby Ladybug van. Then I start to pour.

The caramel oooooozes out so slowly that I'm about to have a heart attack.

"This is taking too long!" I hiss to Marisol who's at the next van over, doing the same thing. She's grabbed one of the wooden spoons that we threw in our backpacks and is spreading the caramel around with it.

"Just get a little on there and smear it around," she says.

I nod and dig the other wooden spoon out of my bag. Finally, I manage to coat the windshield with a thin layer that will take some serious scrubbing to clean off.

When the first windshield is done, I hurry to the next one. Marisol is already ahead of me. Maybe she has a future as a goo artist.

After my third van, a car suddenly swings around the corner. I just have time to duck behind one of the vans as Marisol dives behind a nearby truck. Luckily, the car doesn't slow down. When it's gone, I let my breath out in a long whoosh and rush over to one of the last vans.

"Almost done," I mutter as I uncap the final Tupperware container. The caramel is in mid-ooze when another car swings around the corner. And starts to slow down.

As I scramble to duck behind one of the vans again, I accidentally step in some caramel drippings. My shoe sticks to the ground, and I'm suddenly standing there half barefoot. I scramble to pick up my flip-flop as the car pulls into the parking lot.

Oh holy banana nut bread. It's one of the Ladybug vans.

I abandon my shoe and crouch down behind a nearby van, shoving the wooden spoon and Tupperware back into my bag. Out of the corner of my eye, I see Marisol huddled behind the next one over. We exchange panicked looks as the newly arrived van pulls into a parking spot and the door slides open.

I'm shaking all the way down to my toes, especially the bare toes that don't have a sole under them. What if the driver of the van sees my flip-flop?

"What on earth—?" I hear a woman say. Then she lets out a bunch of swears that are a far cry from my dad's fake ones. Clearly, she's seen the caramel. "Who would do this?"

"I don't know," a guy's voice answers. For some reason, the voice sounds familiar. Come to think of it, so does the woman's.

"I can't believe this," she says. "It'll take hours to clean all of these. We might have to cancel some of our clients tomorrow!"

"It's okay," the guy says. "I'll help."

She lets out a long, pained sigh. "Why does this keep getting harder? I thought expanding into neighboring towns would mean more money for us. Now it's nothing but trouble and time away from my boys."

My stomach dips as I recognize the voice. It's Lillian, the Ladybug owner with the toddler I'd seen in Ryan's Bakery. When I was coming up with my plan, I hadn't thought what it would be like for the person who discovered the caramel. All I cared about was revenge.

"Maybe we should call the police," the guy says.

Marisol and I exchange looks of horror. We have to get out of here *now*.

"I'll go over to the police station," Lillian says. "It's just down the street, and I'm sure they'll want me to fill out a report."

"I'll stay here," the guy says. "In case anyone comes back."

Great. There goes our chance to make a run for it. But we have to. We can't just stay here until the police come.

Marisol must be thinking the same thing because once the woman's footsteps fade, she waves for me to come over to where she is. I take a deep breath and then, as quietly as I can, I army crawl toward her.

"How do we get out of here?" she whispers when I'm huddled beside her.

I grab one of the empty caramel containers. "I'll throw this to distract him and then we run, okay?"

She nods and takes a shaky breath.

I close my eyes and say a silent prayer to every higher power I can think of. Then, on the count of three, I chuck the container as far away from the car as I can. "Go!" I say. And we run.

It's almost impossible to sprint in only one flip-flop, so I kick it aside and take off barefoot. Suddenly, I have déjà vu to when I was chasing after Evan and totally wiped out and flashed him my underwear. I'd do anything to go back to that moment over this one. I'll take mortification over imprisonment any day.

It's only when we're almost out of the parking lot that I glance over my shoulder.

And freeze in place.

Standing on the other side of the parking lot, holding one of my flip-flops in his hand like some confused Prince Charming, is Whit.

At that moment, he turns and looks right at me. And the surprise on his face turns to understanding as he peers down at the shoe in his hand and then at the caramel on the car windows.

"Rachel, come on!" Marisol says, running back toward me. Then she grabs my arm and pulls me down the street, away from Whit who's still standing there, staring back at me like a statue.

Chapter 30

I'm practically hyperventilating by the time we get back to Ryan's Bakery.

"I don't think anyone followed us," says Marisol, jumping on her bike.

I don't move. I can't believe Whit was the one back there. Whit talking to Lillian, as if they were friends. And then I remember what Whit said about living with his sister and about her dropping him off at pastry class on her way to work.

Holy spiced pumpkin. Whit is Lillian's brother. How did I not see it before? They even look alike!

"Rachel, are you crazy?" Marisol cries. "Come on! We have to get out of here."

As if on autopilot, I jump on my bike and start pedaling after her. But my mind is still whirling.

I think of how I told Whit about our plans to prank the Ladybugs, about how I wanted to get revenge for what they'd done to us. And all that time, he knew who the Ladybugs were. He was related to one of them, and he didn't say a word. He even offered to help me get back at them! Probably so that he'd know the plan before it happened and could warn his sister.

No wonder the Ladybugs knew who to strike back at with those online reviews. Whit must have told Lillian everything.

What a mooseheaded jerk.

I can't believe that Evan would think I could like someone like that. I've never hated a person more in my life!

When we get to Marisol's house, I practically collapse on her lawn.

"Well, that was close," she says, panting. "Somehow you lost your shoes, but we got away with it!"

All I can do is stare at my dirty feet. After a second, Marisol notices I'm not saying anything.

"What's wrong?" she asks.

"We didn't get away with it. He saw me. He's probably told the police everything by now."

Marisol's face goes gray. "Who saw us? What are you talking about?"

I tell her about Whit seeing me and how he's bound to tell his sister everything.

Marisol looks toward her house in horror, as if her mom is in there already talking to the police. "Do you think he'd really report us?" she says.

"Yes! Lillian is his sister. Of course he'd take her side!" I put my head in my hands. My mom is going to explode when she hears about this. And if Marisol gets in trouble because she was trying to help me, I'll feel even worse.

"So what do we do?" she says. "Maybe you can talk to Whit and explain things to him. Maybe he hasn't turned us in yet."

"It's too late. Lillian was already at the police station, remember?"

She sighs. "I guess you're right. Well, it doesn't matter what the police do since our parents are going to murder us when they find out. I bet my mom's sharpening her knives right now."

I know she's trying to lighten things up, but it's not helping. Forget the caramel mess we made. The one we've gotten ourselves into is a hundred times stickier.

● ● ●

When I finally slink home, I expect to find Mom sitting in the kitchen waiting for me, ready to shoot fireballs out of her eyes. But instead, she's kneeling on the living room floor, going through a box of old movies that she must have brought down from the attic.

"Oh good, you're home," she says. "What happened to your shoes?" Before I can answer, she shakes her head. "Never mind. Just have a seat for a second."

This is it. Maybe she's only pretending not to be mad, but now she's going to unleash a cruel and unusual punishment on me. I wouldn't be surprised if it involved cow manure. Weirdly, though, she doesn't look angry. Maybe the police haven't called her after all.

I hesitantly perch on the couch. "What's up?"

"I just got off the phone with the real-estate agent, and he kept stressing that it's a seller's market right now." She sighs, like she's been doing nonstop for weeks. "I know you want to stay in this house, Rachel, and I do too, but what he was saying makes a lot of sense." She shakes her head and picks at the carpet.

Wow. I guess she really doesn't know about the goo incident.

"Mom," I say, when it doesn't look like she can go on. "I'm sorry. I know I should be doing more to help you save the business and everything." I thought that the stupid pranks would fix everything. Instead, they've made everything worse. If word gets out about what I did, who'll want to hire us? No one.

"Oh, honey," she says, putting her hand on my knee. "It's not your responsibility. It's mine. We did the best we could, and we'll keep fighting. But it might be time we faced reality and admitted to ourselves that—"

"No!" I cry, jumping to my feet. I can't stand to listen to this right now. "We'll figure it out. We will!" Then, before I break down and admit everything to her, I turn and rush to my room.

My room that might not be my room for much longer.

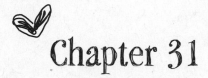

Chapter 31

I lurk outside of Ryan's Bakery on Saturday morning feeling totally delirious. I barely slept all night, waiting for the police to call my mom and tell them what happened. But the phone never rang, so either Whit didn't tell his sister the truth or...I don't know what. Why wouldn't he tell on me? Was he eaten by giant pigeons? One sniff of that caramel, and they went crazy and pecked him to death? Great, now Whit's death by pigeon will be my fault, too.

Relax, I can practically hear Marisol saying. But I can't.

I feel sick to my stomach at the thought of seeing Whit, so I wait until the last possible second to go inside the bakery. But when I get into the kitchen, Whit isn't there.

"Rachel!" Mr. Leroy says, waving me over. "I was afraid I wouldn't have a partner today. Ms. Gomez is away visiting her daughter."

I smile weakly, watching the door, waiting for Whit to come in at any second. At least I won't have to be partners with him today.

Mr. Leroy tells me that he's been practicing a lot, and when I stand back and let him take the lead on the mini fruit tart recipe, I realize he really is doing better. Which is a good thing because I'm so distracted that I can barely pay attention long enough to sift flour. I keep expecting Chef Ryan to yell at me, but he's decided to pick on a couple of college girls on the other side of the room who committed the cardinal sin of using a measuring cup instead of a scale.

"How will you know you have the precise amount of flour if you're not using the proper tools?" he demands.

The girls look ready to cry. I should feel bad for them, but I'm just relieved that they're the ones getting Chef Ryan's wrath for once.

Finally, after what feels like hours, the kitchen door swings open and Whit comes in. For once he isn't wearing his leather jacket, and he looks flustered and sweaty. No sign of giant pigeon beak marks, though.

"Nice of you to join us," Chef Ryan says.

Whit pushes his damp hair off his forehead. "Sorry. Someone put crap all over my sister's minivan. It took me forever to help her clean it off." He shoots a death glare my way and then goes over to a table in the corner to work by himself.

"Rachel?" Mr. Leroy asks. "Are you all right?"

I realize I'm squeezing a pear in my hand so hard that I've bruised it.

"Yeah, sorry," I say. "Um, what's the next step?"

"Is everything all right with you and that boy?" Mr. Leroy asks in a loud whisper. He winks, like he thinks we've had a spat or something. The thought makes my stomach churn.

"No, it isn't. He hates me, and I hate him."

"Huh," he says, rubbing the handful of gray hairs on top of his bald head. "Hate is a pretty strong sentiment. If you ask me, it takes too much energy."

"Well, if he and his sister were trying to ruin your life, you'd hate him, too."

Mr. Leroy gives me a long look. "Sounds like you two have a lot to talk about."

I shake my head. "I'm not talking to him." If I do, I might claw his face off. I turn back to the recipe, trying to make it clear that I don't want to talk about this anymore.

When our fruit tarts are done, I have to admit they're

not bad. Even Chef Ryan doesn't have much to say about them. "Maybe you two should work together more often," he says before moving on to the next team.

Whit's tarts aren't done by the end of class since he came in so late. Chef Ryan clucks like a chicken and shakes his head. "In this business, if you don't focus, you don't succeed," he says.

Whit's jaw tightens so much that I can see it from all the way across the room. "It won't happen again," he says.

"All right," Chef Ryan says to the whole class, clapping his hands like a soccer coach. "Next week, we choose the three finalists who'll go on to the Bake-Off." He shrugs. "Or maybe only two if some of you people don't step up your game." I practically feel him shoot a look my way.

When class is over, I try to rush out of the kitchen, but Mr. Leroy catches my elbow.

"Talk to him," he says, motioning to Whit who's still cleaning up his space. "Trust me."

Mr. Leroy looks so frail and hopeful that I can't say no. What if he has a heart attack because I refuse?

I sigh. "Fine."

When all the other students leave and Chef Ryan is busy washing pans in the back of the room, I go up to Whit and start helping him wipe the counter since I have no idea what else to do.

"Did you come over to apologize?" he says finally.

"Apologize?"

He stops and looks at me. "Yeah. I mean, you and your friend attacked my sister's vans. One of them had so much stuff caked on the windshield that we couldn't get it off. We'll probably have to pay to replace it. Not to mention all the jobs Lillian's employees were late for today because of what you did."

I don't bother pointing out that that was the whole point. "I didn't start all of this," I say. "Your sister's the one who spread rumors about us that weren't true and messed up the flyers that I spent hours putting all around town."

Whit blinks at me. "What are you talking about?"

"Oh, please. Don't play all innocent. The whole reason you wanted to hear about my plan to get back at the Ladybugs was so that you could tell Lillian about it."

He swallows. "Okay, that's kind of true, but only because my sister is having such a hard time. I couldn't let you mess up what she's been working toward for so long."

"What about what my mom and I have been working

toward? Do you have any idea how important this business is to us?"

"Um, yeah." He rolls his eyes. "I think you might have mentioned it, like a million times."

My cheeks burn as I remember how much I've complained to Whit over the past few weeks. What was I thinking, spilling all that stuff to him? "So why didn't you tell your sister that I was involved with the van thing?"

"How do you know I didn't?"

"Because she went to the police. If she knew I was part of it, they would have done something about it."

"I felt bad getting you in trouble," he says, twirling a spoon between his fingers.

"Why do you care?" I say.

He shrugs like it's no big deal.

I should be relieved that he didn't report me to the police—and I am—but I don't understand why he wouldn't. "Come on," I push. "Why didn't you tell your sister?"

Whit shrugs again, but his face turns serious. "Because even though what you did was beyond stupid," he says, "I know you did it because you thought you were helping your mom. If I thought wrecking someone else's stuff might be the only way to help my sister and her family, I'd probably do it, too." He taps the spoon on the counter. "I guess I was trying to help you."

"Help me?" I repeat in disbelief. "You could have helped me by telling me who you were from the beginning, and by not letting me think you were on my side when you're on theirs, and by telling me the truth about the pranks they've been pulling on us. Maybe even warning me!"

"What pranks? What are you talking about?" He's yelling so loudly that Chef Ryan turns from washing pans and shoots us a look across the room. "Okay, yes," he says, lowering his voice. "My sister and I heard some rumors about you guys and kind of jumped on them, but that's it. I swear."

"Yeah, right," I say. "Why should I trust you after everything?"

"Why should I trust *you*?"

We stare at each other with laser-beam hatred.

"Forget it," Whit says finally. "I have to go help my sister fix the mess you made." Then he turns and thunders out of the kitchen.

I stare after him, still furious. Okay, what I did to his sister's vans was bad, definitely worse than I'd planned for it to be, and I'm lucky that Whit pitied me enough not to turn me in. But I can't believe he'd deny everything and keep lying to me! Whit has thought he was better than me—than everyone—since he first walked in here. And the best way to cut him down to size is to win the Bake-Off.

Chapter 32

The next day, after I blow a bunch of my meager savings on ingredients at the grocery store, I have Marisol come over to help me train for the Bake-Off. When she shuffles into my kitchen, I can see from the tight look on her face that she's stressed out. I'm glad to finally have some good news for her.

"I got a message from Evan earlier," I tell her. "He said he found some sound equipment we can use for the Bake-Off."

"Really?" Marisol squeals. "That's perfect! Andrew emailed me this morning and said he can DJ."

"I didn't know he's DJed stuff before."

"He hasn't." She laughs. "But it's better than nothing, right?" Her mood suddenly feels a million times lighter. "Now, what do you want me to do?"

I have her sit at the kitchen table and test my pastry-making skills by choosing random recipes out of a cookbook. We set it up like the Bake-Off so I only have a certain amount of time to get the recipes done. I rush around like a reality-show contestant, desperate to do everything right.

"Hmmm," says Marisol, peering into the cookbook as I'm making banana nut bars. "It says you're supposed to mash the bananas first before you put them into the dry ingredients."

I shrug. "I know, but this way works better. Trust me. I've done it a bunch of times."

Marisol doesn't look convinced, but she leaves it alone. When the entire kitchen is full of baked goods and Marisol's approved them all, I ask my mom to taste test everything. She yums her way through one pastry after another, which makes me feel pretty good.

"I'm sure you'll win," Mom says, but I can tell she's pretty distracted.

After Marisol leaves, I force myself to ask Mom what's wrong, even though I'm afraid I won't like the answer.

"Oh, nothing," she says. "I just…found another job, that's all."

"What? That's great! You won't be working at the law office anymore? Does this one pay better? Will people be nicer to you? When do you start?"

Mom shakes her head. "No, Rachel. I'll still be at the law office, but I'll also be waiting tables a few nights a week at Rib-Eye's."

I gawk at her. "What about the cleaning business?"

"I'll still be doing that, but things have been so slow lately that waiting tables will help bring in the extra money we need to be okay."

I can't believe it. I thought Mom working two jobs was bad enough, but three?

"No, you can't," I say. "Having your own business was your dream. I'll do anything to help. Tell me what I can do."

"Oh, Rachel." She pulls me to her in a sideways hug. "You've already done more than enough. Just keep working hard like you have been. I don't want you dealing with any more stress."

Of course, that's crazy. I'm so stressed all the time that I feel like my muscles could snap at any second like a too-tight string.

"Now," she says. "Marisol told me you're going to be in a fashion show? When did that happen?"

I groan and hide my face. With everything that's been going on in the past few weeks, at least I haven't had time to think about the upcoming horrors of the fashion show.

"My daughter the supermodel," Mom adds, smiling.

It's nice to see her happy, if only for a second. But even if I hopped up and down the runway in a bunny suit, I don't think anything will really make things okay.

The only solution is to beat Whit at the Bake-Off and then find some way to drive the Ladybugs out of town for good.

* * *

That night, for the first time in weeks, I'm desperate to hear my dad's voice. We used to share everything when he still lived with us, but I guess that was bound to change after he left.

"Hey, Roo," he says when he answers the phone. "Long time, no talk. You haven't been returning my calls."

"Sorry. I've been pretty busy." Which is true. But I think part of me has been afraid to talk to him since he announced he might be coming back. What if he suddenly changes his mind and decides to stay in Florida? I have enough disappointment to deal with right now.

"I had to call your mom the other day to make sure you were all right."

"You talked to Mom? Did you tell her about…you know…what you said to me?"

"About coming back? No, not yet. I'm still figuring things out."

"So does that mean it could actually happen?"

"It might," he says. "But that will depend on a few things."

"Like what?"

"I don't really want to get into all of that right now. But I'll come to visit soon, no matter what. Okay?"

"Okay," I say, stifling a sigh. How can talking to one of the people I love most in the world be so frustrating sometimes?

"So I hear you have yourself a boyfriend," Dad says with a teasing tone to his voice.

I suck in a breath. "Oh. Um…"

"Now don't be mad at your mother for telling me. She was so excited that she couldn't help herself."

I chew on my lip. Dad must have talked to her before Evan and I broke up. I open my mouth to tell him the truth, but I can't do it. The words are too hard to say. The truth is, I still don't believe it.

"Roo? Are you there?"

I make a noise that kind of sounds like a grunt.

"Is everything okay? Did you two have a fight?"

"Yeah," I managed to choke out. "I mean, no. I mean…"

I don't know. I don't know anything. I thought Evan

was the perfect guy for me, but maybe he's not. Maybe I'm wrong about him. I feel like everything I've done the past few weeks has been wrong, wrong, wrong.

Chapter 33

The last day of pastry class, I'm jittery from head to toe.

"You'll do fine," Mom says as she drops me off. "I'll come get you after class and we'll go out to celebrate." Since we only have two cleaning jobs today, Mom is going to do them while I'm in class. How depressing to think that only two months ago, our Saturdays and our Thursday nights were packed with clients. And now, thanks to the Ladybugs, we have almost none.

That reminder is all the fuel I need to march into class, ready to kick Whit's butt.

When I get there, Whit is already wearing his apron and stretching his arms and legs like he's about to run some kind of weird baking race.

"Where's your leather jacket?" I can't help shooting at him.

His mouth tightens. "I got caramel all over it when I was cleaning my sister's van," he says.

Oh. I don't know what to say, so I grab my apron and pull it on. I focus on trying to breathe and concentrate.

"It was my dad's," Whit says after a second.

"What?"

He comes up beside me and lowers his voice. "The jacket. It was my dad's. It's pretty much the only thing I have of his."

I open my mouth and close it again. Holy deviled eggs. What am I supposed to say to that? His dad died and left him the jacket, and now because of me, it's ruined?

"Rachel!" someone calls across the room. I spot Mr. Leroy waving at me. Still speechless, I practically run away from Whit. Maybe I should have apologized to him about his father's jacket, but I guess it's too late now. Besides, I have to concentrate on qualifying for the Bake-Off, not feeling bad about something that I can't fix.

In fact, I bet Whit told me about that at this moment to throw me off my game. For all I know, he made up the whole thing about the jacket being his dad's to mess with me!

"I didn't think you'd be competing today," I say to Mr. Leroy.

He slowly rolls up his sleeves. "I'm not vying for a spot

in the Bake-Off, but I figured I should at least show off what I've learned."

Beside him, Ms. Gomez is carefully putting her utensils in order like they're surgical tools. Normally, people are chatting and laughing before class, but today they're quiet and focused. I guess Chef Ryan's made everyone feel competitive. Realizing that other people are taking this seriously makes me even more nervous.

Then Chef Ryan comes in and announces that we'll start in a minute. I don't have time to be nervous anymore. It's time to get to work.

"To challenge you," Chef Ryan says, "I'll be giving you a brand-new recipe and seeing what you do with it. Those of you who advance to the Bake-Off tomorrow will be asked to make one of the pastries we've already made during the class." He grins evilly. "Though, tomorrow, you won't be given a copy of the instructions. You'll have to work from memory."

I swallow as he grabs a stack of papers and passes them out.

"And today we're making molten chocolate cake," he announces.

I hear people groan around me. It's not a tricky recipe,

but it's hard to get the inside of the cake perfectly melty. I can't help grinning, though, since it's one of my favorite things to make.

I quickly glance at the recipe before going to grab everything I'll need. I could make this without even looking at the instructions at all, but I don't want to mess it up, especially not when Chef Ryan is watching each of us like a hawk.

As I get to work, I can hear Mr. Leroy humming at the table next to mine. I think he's the only person who's actually enjoying himself. Everyone else looks as stressed out as I feel.

But the further I get into the recipe, the more relaxed I am. The familiar smells of chocolate and butter calm me down, and after a few minutes, I realize I'm almost having fun.

When the timer goes off, I'm actually surprised to discover that there are other people around me. For the first time since I started this class, I was able to relax and just enjoy the process. Isn't that the reason I signed up for this class in the first place?

Chef Ryan goes down the row army-style again, and this time I'm actually pretty proud of the dessert standing in front of me. As I glance around at the others, I see a few cakes whose centers have already erupted and others that are obviously rock hard. I have to admit that Whit's looks pretty good, but no better than mine.

As Chef Ryan gets closer to my dessert, I start to get really nervous. He digs his spoon into the cake and pops a tiny bite into his mouth. The chocolate center oozes out onto the plate just like it's supposed to. He chews it slowly, like he's swishing a sip of wine around.

Finally, he swallows and says, "Good job, Rachel." Then he moves on to the next person.

My legs suddenly go watery under me. He liked it. He actually liked it! And he told me I'd done a good job! No criticism. No yelling. Nothing!

Finally, when he's made his way all the way down the line, Chef Ryan looks over his notes and then clears his throat. "And the three finalists are…" He glances at his list again. "Adam Whitney, Rachel Lee, and Gordon Leroy."

Whit lets out a whoop at the other side of the room, while I grin so wide it feels like my lips might curl backward over my face. Mr. Leroy, meanwhile, wipes tears from his wrinkled eyes. "My wife would be so proud," he says when he sees me looking at him. Then he turns to

Chef Ryan and I know he's about to tell him that he won't be competing in the Bake-Off. But before he can get out a word, I jump in front of him.

"Please, Mr. Leroy," I say softly, "come to the Bake-Off, okay? You deserve to be there. Your wife wouldn't want you to be home alone missing her." I don't know where these words are coming from. Or maybe I do. After Dad left, I did nothing but mope, wishing he was still around. The only way I got out of that funk was by actually doing something about it.

Mr. Leroy gives me a watery smile. "All right," he says. "I suppose I can give it a try."

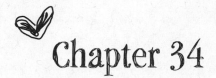

Chapter 34

The morning of the Bake-Off, my nerves are making me so sick to my stomach that I'm about to throw up everything I've ever eaten in my whole life. Thankfully, Mom is there to speak to me in soft, relaxing tones and practically force-feed me dry toast.

"You'll do fine," she says. "You have every one of those recipes memorized backward and forward and upside down. And I'll be sitting in the front row, cheering you on."

"Is Mr. Hammond coming?" I ask.

Mom frowns. "Robert is…" She doesn't finish, like she can't come up with a good excuse for why he won't be there.

"Look, Mom. It's probably none of my business what's going on with you and Mr. Hammond, but he's a really nice guy. If you have to be with someone other than Dad, he's not a bad choice."

"I know that."

"Then why are you ditching him? Did he do something wrong?"

"I'm…trying to be more independent."

"By never seeing him? By not answering his calls? I'm not an expert, but I'm pretty sure that's not the way to show a guy that you like him."

Mom sighs. "I know. I just don't want to put us in the same situation all over again."

"You won't. Even if things don't work out with Mr. Hammond, we'll be fine. But for now, I think you should keep him around, especially when he makes you smile so much."

And then a miracle happens. She does smile, *really* smile, for the first time in weeks. "Look at you, Miss Smarty. You can bake *and* you have brains!"

The mention of baking makes my stomach lurch. I groan. "Maybe I shouldn't go to the Bake-Off. What if I'm really sick?"

"You were feeling fine a second ago," Mom points out. "Besides, if you skip the Bake-Off, Marisol will—"

"Never forgive me," I finish. "I know. Okay, fine. I'll go." I groan again and get to my feet. "But if I lose the

Bake-Off because I gave the judges the plague, I'm blaming you."

* * *

When Mom drops me off at Ryan's Bakery, she plants a good-luck kiss on my forehead and says, "I'll go pick up Robert and be back in a few minutes." She hasn't stopped smiling since our conversation this morning, which is a good sign. Too bad I'm still ready to throw up.

As soon as I get out of the car, I'm struck by what an amazing job Marisol did in planning the whole event. There's a stage set up in the parking lot for the music and fashion show, and lots of people are already milling around. I go into the bakery where everyone is furiously prepping, including Chef Ryan and Cherie, who both look thrilled at how busy things are. Then I wander into the kitchen where the Bake Off will be. Someone's set up cameras that will record the action and project it onto a screen above the stage outside.

It hits me that people are going to be watching every move I make. My stomach does a flip, and I turn and run toward the bathroom. As I dart past, I spot Briana and Angela standing in the corner, clearly having an argument.

I have to smile when I notice that Angela is wearing her

favorite T-shirt. I guess that means she found it under her bed. Marisol will be relieved. I think that prank still gives her nightmares.

I'm about to round the corner when I hear Briana say my name, and I freeze. The churning in my stomach fades as I creep behind a nearby rack of pots and pans and try to listen to their conversation.

"You mean you just took it?" Briana is saying. "That necklace belongs to Caitlin. You had no right to steal it."

"I didn't steal it!" Angela says. "She didn't want it anymore, and I did. She's not your best friend now. I am. Why should she have it when she doesn't even wear it anymore?"

"That's not the point!" says Briana. "How did you even get it?"

Angela shrugs. "I snuck into her room when Caitlin's mom was outside doing yard work. It wasn't a big deal."

Briana shakes her head like she can't believe what she's hearing. That makes two of us.

"You're a total psycho, you know that?" she says. "I thought it was bad enough that you were stalking me, but you've been breaking into people's houses and stealing their stuff? Especially after you accused everyone in the world of stealing that ugly shirt when it was in your room the whole time? You really are crazy."

"I'm not crazy!" Angela insists. "I've wanted to be friends with you since first grade. Do you think I was just going to give up my chance?"

Briana shakes her head. Then she seems to spot me out of the corner of her eye. I'm standing there with my mouth hanging open, trying to process what I just heard. Angela was the one who stole Caitlin's necklace?

I expect Briana to snarl at me, to ask me if I have a staring problem, but instead she grabs Angela's arm and drags her over to me. "Tell her," she says.

Angela stares at Briana like she's the one who's crazy. "What?"

"Tell Rachel what you did," she says.

"The necklace," I whisper. "You took it."

"Not just that," says Briana. "She messed up your flyers, too."

"What? Why?"

Angela huffs and doesn't respond.

"Because," Briana finally answers for her, "she knew I was mad at you about the Caitlin thing and she thought I'd be impressed if she did something to get back at you. As if writing 'sux' on something would ever impress me. As if I even care about your stupid cleaning business."

My blood feels like it's turning into a bubbling stew. "Do you know what you've done?" I ask Angela, my voice taking on the scary calm tone that my mom uses when she's furious. I can't believe it. All the pranks Marisol and I pulled. All the things I accused Whit and Lillian of. And none of it was the Ladybugs' fault.

"Rachel Lee?" I hear Cherie call out. "Has anyone seen Rachel Lee?" When she spots me, she rushes over with a clipboard in hand. "Oh good, you're here. We're starting in five minutes. We need you in the kitchen right now."

But I don't care about the Bake-Off. My eyes are still zeroed in on Angela. She's the reason my life has gotten totally derailed.

"You're a horrible person, you know that?" I spit at her. "Because of you, my mom's business is ruined and things with Evan are…" I can't even get the words out. They hurt too much. Instead, I stomp over and get right in Angela's face. "Why would you do that to me?"

She looks terrified, like she thinks I might hit her. "I didn't do anything to you," she whispers. "I just did what I had to do."

My breath stops in my throat.

"Rachel!" Cherie says. "We need you on stage right now."

I'm shaking as Cherie pulls me away from Angela and walks me toward the stage.

I did what I had to do. Those are pretty much the exact words I said to Whit when I was justifying the Ladybug pranks. I was convinced I had no choice, that this was the only way to keep things from changing. That to keep my life from falling apart, I had to sink as low as necessary.

Maybe that's what Angela was doing, too.

Chapter 35

As Chef Ryan explains the Bake-Off rules, I can barely pay attention. I'm not even distracted by the video cameras set up nearby. All I can think about is what Angela did, and how that made everything spiral totally out of control.

And because of her stupid decisions, I made a bunch of stupid ones of my own. And now Evan hates me, Whit hates me, and my mom's business is all but dead in the water.

"Ready?" Chef Ryan says.

I blink, realizing we're about to start. I glance at Whit on one side of me, looking ready to run a marathon, and then at Mr. Leroy on the other side. He seems so relaxed that he could be in his own kitchen at home.

Focus, I tell myself. Forget about Angela and the Ladybugs and everything, and focus.

Chef Ryan riffles around in the hat of recipes, just like

he did in class the other day. Then he pulls out a slip of paper and reads: "Caramel squares."

My stomach sinks all the way through my legs and into the floor. Of all the desserts that fate could have thrown my way, why does it have to be the one I messed up the worst in class?

But you did great at home, a small voice in the back of my mind chimes in. *The caramel squares you made last time were amazing.* It takes me a second to realize that the small voice sounds a lot like Evan.

I take a deep breath and get to work. Around me, Whit and Mr. Leroy are scurrying around like mice, but I try to block them out as I grab all the ingredients and bring them back to my table.

I keep running over the recipe in my head, even though I could recite it in my sleep. I don't want to accidentally skip a step because I'm nervous.

As I start measuring things out, I can't help thinking of the caramel that Marisol and I dumped on the Ladybug vans. How did things get so messed up? Why was I convinced that doing that stupid stuff was the only solution?

Rachel, you have to focus, the Evan voice says.

Out of the corner of my eye, I spot Whit mixing

ingredients. How is he already ahead of me? When he catches me peering at him, he quickly looks away.

He has every right to hate me, I realize. After everything I did to him and his sister, after everything I accused him of. Okay, so the Ladybugs jumped on the rumor Angela started, but that's the only bad thing they did to us. Now, because of me, Whit lost his father's jacket and Lillian might have to give up part of her business.

I'm so distracted that I almost drop a bowl of sugar.

Forget about all that, the Evan voice says. *You can't do anything about it now.*

But…

Pretend you're at home. Just relax and pretend you're doing all this for yourself.

I try to picture Marisol sitting nearby on a kitchen stool, chatting with me like she always does when I'm baking. I can do this. I know I can. It's not about the competition. It's about doing something I love.

I pause for a second, realizing that it's true. Even if Chef Ryan thinks I'll never be good enough, even if I don't win this competition, even if I never become a pastry chef, it won't change the fact that I love baking.

But that doesn't mean I always know what I'm doing

or always know how to do it perfectly. That's where Chef Ryan was right. I've been so set on doing things my way that I've been totally deaf to any criticism. It's time to stop being stubborn and be open to change for once in my life.

"Rachel?" I hear Chef Ryan say. "Are you okay?" He's peering at me with a look of total concern on his face.

Of course he's worried. I'm standing here in front of my mixing bowl, staring off into space. Apparently, I can't bake and think at the same time.

"I'm fine." I suck in a deep breath and get back to work. Instead of using the recipe as a general guideline like I usually do, I follow it step by step. I'm tempted to take shortcuts, to do things my way, but I ignore those impulses and do everything by the book.

The minutes tick, tick, tick by, but I barely pay attention to the clock. Before I know it, my squares are in the oven and it's time to make the chocolate glaze. Even though I could make it in my sleep, I still go over the recipe carefully in my head and realize that the way Chef Ryan does it might actually take less time than my method.

Who knew?

Well, I guess he did. And Marisol had an inkling when

she reminded me that a professional chef might be able to teach me a few things.

As I melt the butter, I can't get over how stubborn I've been. Clinging to my parents' marriage, desperate to keep the house, terrified of anything changing—even the way I hold my spatula! And because I was so petrified of change, I was willing to do anything to keep my life from getting even more out of my control. Which included dragging Marisol into totally crazy plans and not being honest with Evan.

No wonder everything went so wrong.

Ding!

The oven timer goes off, and I rush over to get my caramel squares. I can practically feel Chef Ryan's eyes on me as I cut up the squares with my spatula. Just the way he taught me. And, sure enough, it works perfectly.

I have just enough time to get one of the squares on a plate and pour a little chocolate glaze on top before the buzzer goes off and the competition is over. Before I have a chance to taste my dish.

Uh-oh. Suddenly, all I can think about are the horrible soap cookies I brought to Evan's house. If only I'd tried those beforehand, I could have averted total disaster.

I'm panting as I step away from my dessert. My food

looks pretty good, but for all I know, it could taste awful or be full of rat poison. I wish I'd had one more second to sample it.

I glance over at Whit's plate and have to bite back a smile. His caramel square is lopsided and his chocolate glaze looks watery. Maybe I have a chance to win this thing, after all.

Then I turn in the other direct and almost gasp at the sight of Mr. Leroy's dessert. Not only does it look perfectly made, but he's drizzled the chocolate glaze in the shape of a heart. His dessert looks the best out of the three of ours. If it tastes anywhere near as good as it looks, I'm in serious trouble.

Chapter 36

Before Chef Ryan announces the winners, he makes a long speech to the TV audience about how happy he is that everyone came and how great our class has been. I want to laugh, remembering how miserable he seemed most of the time.

Then again, he looks genuinely proud of us today. Maybe we've turned out better than he expected.

But suddenly, I stop listening to his speech because I spot someone peeking into the doorway of the kitchen. It's Evan. And if I'm not hallucinating, he's holding a guitar.

What the Shrek?

When he sees me looking at him, he ducks behind the door frame and disappears.

As Chef Ryan marches down the line of desserts and comments on each one for the camera, my mind is racing. Does this mean Evan isn't furious with me anymore? Or did he finally find a way to get over his fear of playing in front of people? I doubt he's wandering around with a guitar for no reason.

Finally, Chef Ryan clears his throat and says: "And the results are in!"

I close my eyes.

"In third place is...Adam Whitney!"

My eyes fly open. I glance over at Whit who does his best to smile, but I can tell he's disappointed. I can't say I blame him. Okay, so he's pretty full of himself when it comes to baking, but then again, I have been, too.

"In second place is...Rachel Lee!"

I realize that I'm not surprised about losing, not at all, not after seeing Mr. Leroy's dessert. And weirder still, I'm not even all that upset. All along, I've been determined to beat Whit to prove to him (and maybe to myself) that I'm good enough to be here. But Mr. Leroy has worked hard all summer. If anyone deserves to win, it's him.

"And that means our winner is...Gordon Leroy!"

Mr. Leroy steps forward, his eyes shining behind his thick glasses, and accepts his prize: fifty dollars and a gift certificate for more cooking classes. When he glances over at me, he looks completely overwhelmed. I reach out and squeeze his hand.

"Your wife would be really proud of you," I say.

Mr. Leroy nods, clearly too emotional to say anything. And that's when something hits me, like lightning zapping my brain. What if I'd just asked Evan about our relationship all those weeks ago? What if I'd come out and told him I wanted him to be my boyfriend? What if I hadn't let my stupid paranoia about us totally paralyze me and I'd been up front with him about how I feel?

Before I realize what I'm doing, I go up to Chef Ryan and whisper, "Can I borrow this for a second?" Then, not giving him time to object, I pull the microphone out of his hand and go to stand in front of the nearest camera. Clearly, I've seen too many movies where people do big, romantic gestures in public.

I'm shaking from head to toe, but it has nothing to do with the audience that I know is watching. All I care about is that Evan is out there and that he might still feel the same way about me that I feel about him.

"Um, hi," I say. "Um." I swallow what feels like a hairball in my throat. "Evan? Evan Riley? If you're watching, which I think you are because I think I just saw you? If you're watching, I have to tell you that I, um...I'm sorry. I should have told you how I felt from the beginning. I'm sorry I messed everything up. I swear that I don't like anyone else. Why would I? I mean, you're perfect for me. You're like my..." My brain stalls for a second. "My penguin."

Oh my goldfish. Is "penguin" the only word my brain can ever come up with?

I hold the microphone for a minute longer, not sure what else to say. "Sincerely, Rachel Lee," I finally mumble, because apparently my brain is full of not only penguins but also letter-writing tips. I hurry to give Chef Ryan the mic back before my brain decides to spout my bra size or something.

If this was a movie, Evan would come running into the kitchen and sweep me into a kiss. But, of course, this is my non-Hollywood life, so nothing happens. Chef Ryan thanks everyone for coming and tells them to stay tuned for the fashion show, which will start in fifteen minutes. Then he thanks the businesses that helped sponsor the event, including—sure enough—Ladybug Cleaners.

When I hear the name, I feel deflated all over again. How can I ever make things right with Whit and his sister and the other Ladybugs?

Once the cameras are shut off, Chef Ryan hands me my second-place prize, which is a gift certificate for another class at the bakery.

I stare at it for a moment. "Are you sure you want me to come back?"

He smiles. "If you keep baking like you did today, I might even let you teach a class."

Then he hurries off toward the back office, probably worn out from having to be nice to so many people. But his words leave a warm, gooey feeling in my chest. Maybe I haven't been kidding myself all this time after all.

● ● ●

As the camera people start moving their stuff to set up for the fashion show outside, I spot Lillian and a couple other Ladybugs coming into the kitchen carrying cleaning supplies. I guess they're going to take care of the mess we made while we were baking.

As Lillian gives Whit an I'm-proud-of-you hug, I head toward them, knowing I need to apologize.

"Congrats," he says when he spots me. "Your dessert was way better than mine."

"Thanks," I say. "I'm glad Mr. Leroy won, though."

Whit nods. "Yeah, I guess I am, too."

I look back and forth between Whit and Lillian. Saying I'm sorry has never been my thing, but considering how many times I've had to do it in the past few months, I'm starting to be a pro.

"So I owe you both a huge apology. I was the one who poured that stuff all over your vans. I'm so, so, so sorry. I'll pay for any damages. I promise."

Lillian looks surprised, but she nods slowly.

"And I'm sorry about your dad's jacket," I tell Whit, "and about all the other stupid stuff I did. I was convinced you guys were out to get me and my mom, but it turns out that someone else was messing with me. I'm sorry I blamed you. I'll take down all the bad reviews I posted online. And if I can help you get the jacket fixed, I will."

Lillian and Whit exchange a look. "Thank you," she says finally. "I appreciate your offer."

"If it makes any difference," I add, "I had nothing to do with that necklace being stolen."

Lillian looks suddenly embarrassed. "I know. I overheard your conversation with Angela before the Bake-Off. I apologize for eavesdropping, but more than that, I apologize for ever repeating that rumor in the first place. If it helps, I'll make sure to tell everyone that you had nothing to do with the thefts. Maybe then we can safely put all this behind us?"

I nod eagerly. "That would be great." Maybe my mom won't ever have to know about the whole stupid prank war.

"One more thing," Whit says, peering down at his shoes. "I'm the one who posted those reviews about you. My sister wouldn't do it, so I…" He clears his throat. "I'll take them down, I promise. It was stupid of me to even…"

He doesn't finish, but he doesn't need to. I totally understand.

"It's okay." I want to add that we're even, but I know we're definitely not. I turn back to Lillian. "I can come work off some of the money I owe you, if you want. I remember you said you wanted more time to spend with your kids."

She sighs and puts her arm around Whit. "I think we've decided to cut down on the clients we have around here. I thought expanding into neighboring towns would help business, but it turns out it's too much for us to handle."

"Really?" I should be glad since that means Mom and I might have more work again, but I feel bad that they're retreating because of all the trouble I caused them.

Whit shrugs and says, "We gave it a shot, right?" And I must admit that in that moment, I don't hate him at all.

Lillian gives me a warm smile and then heads off to start cleaning.

"I still feel bad about your jacket," I tell Whit. "I want to make it up to you somehow."

His face brightens. "I have an idea. How about you show me how to make your chocolate glaze. Mine came out gross."

"Deal." I stick out my hand to shake on it, but Whit's looking past me at something.

I turn and spot Evan standing in the doorway. Of course, he had to come in during the one minute that Whit and I are actually getting along.

"Sorry," I tell Whit. "I, um, have to—"

"I totally understand," he says. "Go get your penguin."

Chapter 37

H ey," I say to my penguin.

"Hey," he says.

We stare at each other for way longer than is comfortable, even for penguins.

"So, um, did you decide to play?" I finally ask. "I thought I saw you with your guitar."

"Oh, yeah. I'm supposed to do a couple songs during the fashion show. I realized I was being a total wimp. I mean, if you can bake in front of a bunch of people even though it scares you, and if you can get up and model aprons after that, then I don't have an excuse."

I groan. "I totally forgot about the fashion show." I can hear music echoing from outside. No doubt Marisol will come get me any second and throw an apron on me, which means that I need to say what I'm going to say now, before I run out of time. "So, um…I meant what I said," I blurt out. "Not about the penguin part because that doesn't make any sense, but—"

"Actually, it kind of does. Once a penguin finds its perfect other penguin, they stay together pretty much forever."

I blink at him. "Really?"

Evan nods. "Yeah. I remember reading that somewhere."

"Oh." Maybe my brain isn't totally useless after all, because that is exactly how I feel about him.

"So, you really aren't into Whit?" he asks.

"No, not at all. I'm into you."

Evan's face lights up, and in that moment I can see that he never stopped liking me. So I do something I never, ever, ever thought I would *ever* do. I lean in and I kiss him.

Okay, it's only on the cheek. But hey, baby steps, right?

Even brushing my lips against his cheek is enough to make my whole body tingle.

When I step back, he's grinning back at me like he just won the lottery. I'm totally speechless but in a good way, for once.

Of course Marisol chooses that moment to come rushing up to me.

"There you are!" she says, throwing an apron over my neck. I can tell she's trying to ignore the fact that Evan and

I are obviously back together, but her grin tells me she's as happy as I am.

"You guys have five minutes before you're both on, okay?" she says. "And thanks again for coming, Evan. We can really use the help. I mean, Andrew's doing the best he can, but..." She rolls her eyes as "Monster Mash" starts playing outside, but I can tell she's thrilled to have her own penguin back in town.

She waggles her eyebrows at me and then rushes off to wrangle Whit into his apron.

Evan takes my hand and walks me to where the other models are lining up. I can feel him shaking, which means he's as nervous as I am.

"You'll be great," I tell him.

He smiles. "You too."

As he goes to take his position at the edge of the stage, I notice Andrew Ivanoff in the back of the crowd, wearing headphones and DJing the event. He looks totally stressed out. His entire head is so pink that it reminds me of a watermelon. It's definitely a good thing Evan came, for lots of reasons.

I also spot Evan's three friends from the other night sitting in the audience. Yesterday, I would have been mortified at the sight of them, but today I feel okay. Yes, I almost poisoned them, but it was an accident. And now that I know for sure that I'm a good chef, I'll have to ask Evan to set up another time for all of us to hang out so I can wow them with a non-soapy recipe.

Marisol comes up and welcomes everyone, and the fashion show starts. Then Evan plays a few chords. His eyes are closed and he looks so pale that his skin is actually kind of bluish. But he keeps strumming on the guitar, and after a second, he starts singing. His voice is soft but clear, and the song starts to get faster and faster so that it has a strong beat for us to walk to.

As Ms. Gomez sashays across the stage in a pink apron, I'm barely thinking about having to strut my stuff in front of everyone. I'm too busy beaming with pride at how great Evan sounds, especially when he seems to get more comfortable and his voice grows louder. After a minute, he even opens his eyes and glances out at the audience.

Whit heads out on the stage in his apron, and I take a deep breath, knowing I'm next. But as I peer out at the crowd, I spot my mom and Mr. Hammond sitting in the front row. And beside them is…my dad?

I stumble back, and my eyes blur like they can't process what they're seeing. But before I can react, someone taps me on the shoulder and whispers, "You're on."

My brain is still swimming as I step out onto the stage, keeping my eyes on my dad. What is he doing here? Why didn't he tell me he was coming? Did Mom know he was going to be here? Is he staying for good? Is he—

Suddenly, I realize I'm not on stage anymore. Miraculously, I made it across without wiping out or embarrassing myself. I was so busy obsessing about my dad being here that I barely even noticed my legs moving. So much for my big modeling debut. I sleepwalked right through it.

I stand on the other side of the stage, half listening to Evan playing and half watching my dad enjoying the show. I'm so excited to hug him that my body actually aches.

Finally, the fashion show is over and Evan finishes his second song. The crowd goes nutso. Everyone cheers when Marisol comes out to take a bow, and they cheer again when she points to Evan and he gives a little bob of his head.

I'm so happy for both of them that my chest feels like it's about to burst. Even Chef Ryan is grinning like crazy. I guess that means the event was a huge success.

When it's finally over, everyone starts milling around and chatting. I give Evan a huge hug and tell him how great he did.

"Thanks to you," he says.

"Me?"

"I was about to give up and run off the stage, but then I heard this voice in the back of my head, telling me I was doing fine. It sounded just like you."

I gawk at him. "I…I heard you in my head, too, during the Bake-Off. Do you think we're psychically connected or something?"

He shrugs. "Maybe. Either way, I think we have each other to thank for rocking it." He grins. "You looked like a real model out there!"

I roll my eyes, unbelievably relieved it's over.

The whole time I'm talking to him, my eyes keep wandering to where my dad is talking to my mom and Mr. Hammond. Evan must notice that I'm distracted because he asks: "Is that your dad?"

I nod. "He must have just flown up. I had no idea he was going to be here."

"Then go see him!" says Evan. "But after that, make sure to come back so my friends can say congrats. They can't believe they ate soap cookies made by someone famous."

I give him another hug and then I rush off the stage toward my dad, who's waiting for me with his arms wide open.

Chapter 38

Rachel Roo!" Dad cries, squeezing me so tightly that I almost start coughing. "I can't believe how much I've missed you."

"I know," I say into his shoulder. "I missed you, too."

Finally, he pulls away and I can see tears in the corners of his eyes. "I was so proud of you when you were up there. And second place in the baking competition! Wowee!"

At that moment my mom comes over and wraps me in a hug of her own. "You were wonderful, Rachel."

I'm practically bursting from all the love. Then I notice that Mr. Hammond is hanging back, as if he doesn't want to intrude on a family moment.

"What are you doing here?" I ask Dad in a low voice.

He and Mom exchange a look before he says, "I wanted to surprise you."

"So does this mean you're back for good now?"

Before he can answer, Lillian appears next to me, still wearing her Ladybug apron. "Sorry to interrupt," she says. "Rachel, is this your mother?"

"Oh, yeah. Um, Mom, this is Lillian. She owns Ladybug Cleaners."

My mom blinks in surprise. She knows the Ladybugs are new in town, but that's about it. She has no idea how involved I've been in their business and why I even know Lillian in the first place.

"It's so nice to meet you," Lillian says, shaking Mom's hand. "I was wondering if I could talk to you for a minute?"

"Of course," Mom answers. She still looks a little confused, but she follows Lillian to the end of the row, leaving me and Dad alone.

"Look, Roo," he says. "I'm sorry if I got your hopes up, but—"

"But you're not coming back," I finish.

He shakes his head and gives me a sad smile. "Ellie just helped me get a job teaching scuba lessons through the resort where she works. Things are finally starting to come together in Florida. I can't give up without giving them a real shot, you know? Even though I wish I wasn't so far away from you."

I should feel disappointed, but the truth is, I think part of me has been expecting this. I love my dad, but with him, seeing is believing. And even though I'm seeing him right now, it's still hard to believe he's here.

"I wish you weren't so far away, either," I say.

"You'll just have to come visit! How about next month before school starts? We'd have so much fun."

It does sound fun, even though leaving Evan behind for part of the summer will be kind of hard. But I have a feeling that he and I will be a lot better at communicating with each other from now on.

As my family and I go to leave, I spot Briana standing with a few other people. One of them is Angela, of course, but I'm surprised when I realize the other two are Caitlin Schubert and Steve Mueller. Funny how I used to have serious butterflies in my stomach every time I saw Steve, and now looking at him does nothing for me.

I'm surprised that Caitlin and Briana are talking normally instead of arguing like they were the last time I saw them. Then Briana motions to Angela, who reaches into her pocket and pulls out something that she hands over to Caitlin.

When Caitlin looks down at the object in her hand, she

smiles and I realize that it must be the friendship necklace Angela stole. After a second, she hangs it around her neck and then throws her arms around Briana. The two of them are so busy with their happy reunion that they don't seem to notice when Angela storms off, clearly furious.

As I'm about to turn away, I spot something that makes my mouth sag almost all the way to the floor: Briana turning and giving Whit a smile across the room. And, weirder still, Whit smiling back at her! Marisol and I joked about Whit and Angela being perfect for each other, but maybe Whit and Briana would make more sense. He might be the only guy able to stand up to her, and after all she's been through, Briana might actually appreciate having someone to count on again. Not that I'll ever think she's a wonderful person, but maybe she deserves to be happy, too.

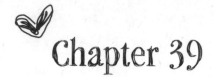

Chapter 39

That night, after Dad goes to stay with a friend of his for the night, Marisol and I chat on the phone for an hour, rehashing every up and down of the Bake-Off (which I know she'll be gushing about for months). When we're done going over every detail, I tear up the Prank List and throw it away. Knowing it's gone makes me feel lighter already.

"Can you do me a favor?" I ask Marisol. "Next time I ask you to dump something on someone's car, can you smack me and tell me I'm an idiot?"

She laughs and promises that she will. "So listen," she says. "I should thank you."

"For what? Didn't we just agree that I've been a total idiot?"

"True, but you also told me to give my mom and Andrew a chance to get to know each other. And you know what? I think she might be coming around. The three of us went out for ice cream after the Bake-Off, and she seemed to like him."

"Does this mean he's officially your boyfriend now?" I ask, suddenly giddy.

"Not exactly, but I think we're getting there. I'd say we're a work in progress."

It's my turn to laugh. "Aren't we all?"

"So tomorrow," Marisol says, "I think you have to draw part of the mural."

"Are you kidding? Do you want your room covered with blobby stick figures?"

She laughs. "If they come from you, then yes. I don't want it to be my mural. It should be ours."

"But you know I'm not an artist!"

"You also said you weren't a model, and you proved yourself wrong, didn't you?"

"Okay, you asked for it," I say, but I'm smiling. We both know my artistic skills are worse than most monkeys', but the fact that Marisol thinks I can do it is good enough for me. Besides, maybe art is like baking. The more you do it, the better you get at it, especially if you can learn to stop being a stubborn poopy head.

After we hang up, I glance over at the box of things from the attic that is still sitting in the corner of my room where Mom put it weeks ago. I guess I can't put off going through it for much longer.

But I don't think I can deal with doing it alone. So I grab the box and bring it out to the living room where Mom is, shockingly, watching an old episode of *Pastry Wars*. When she sees me staring, she laughs and says, "I think that Bake-Off today got me hooked!" Then she glances at the box in my arms. "Do you need some help?"

Even though I know she's asking if I need help carrying it—which I don't—I still nod. "I don't think I can go through this stuff by myself."

Mom's face softens, and she nods as I put the box in the middle of the living room floor.

"Ready?" she says when we're both poised over it.

I nod, even though I'm not sure I am. At least doing this with her is a million times better than doing it by myself.

When we open the box, I expect to feel the same rush of panic and sadness that I did the first time. Instead, it's strangely comforting to see all those old pictures and drawings and report cards.

"I had an interesting conversation earlier," Mom says

as we start sorting everything into piles. "With Lillian at Ladybug Cleaners."

My stomach drops. With everything that happened today, I forgot about Lillian pulling my mom away after the fashion show. "What did she say?" Did Lillian tell her about all the stuff I did to the Ladybugs? She said she wanted to put everything behind us, but what if she changed her mind?

"Oh nothing much. We just talked about the possibility of merging our cleaning businesses." Mom laughs at what must be total shock on my face. "I know it's sudden, but she said she got the idea after she spoke with you today. She knew we were looking for more clients, and she's been having a hard time staying on top of working and being a mom, so she suggested we team up. Lee Cleaners would become part of Ladybug Cleaners, and we'd help each other out."

"What about your business?" I say. "You've always wanted to be your own boss."

"And I still would be, only with a co-owner. To be honest, I think this could be the perfect solution. I like being my own boss, but I don't think I'm cut out for the stress of doing everything on my own. Plus, Lillian's already been doing this for a few years. She knows how everything runs, and she can teach me a lot. The only thing is…"

"What?"

"Well," says Mom, brushing her hair off her forehead. "For this to work, I would have to quit my office job. I don't think I'd have time to do both."

"Really?" I squeal. "That's great!" Then I realize why my mom looks so worried. Her job at the law office is the stable one she's had for years. Thanks to that job, we've always at least had money for food and clothes. Without it, who knows what will happen?

"So before I decide anything, we'll have to sit down and talk this through," Mom says.

I stare down at the picture I drew when I was a kid, the one with my parents and my imaginary turtle standing in front of our house. When I was little, I thought I'd live here forever, but I also thought that my parents (and my invisible turtle) would never go anywhere. I guess some things have to change, no matter what.

"Mom, I think we should sell the house."

She drops a stack of report cards and stares at me in surprise. "But you love this place."

"I know, but I love you more. And I don't want you to have to give up your business because of this house, or to work a million jobs so we can afford to stay here."

Mom wipes her eyes. "Are you sure?"

"As long as we don't have to live with Aunt Nelly in Connecticut, okay?"

She smiles. "Don't worry about that. I've already started looking at some apartments around here so we can stay in town. I realized that moving away would just make both of us miserable."

I let out a little whoop of joy and throw my arms around her. "Thank you!"

I'm practically whistling with glee when I go back to cleaning out the box. It barely even seems like a chore anymore.

"We don't have to get rid of any of this if you don't want to," Mom says when she sees me paging through my fifth-grade yearbook.

"I'm sure most of it can go. But yeah, maybe keeping some of it is a good idea. Like Mr. Hip. I don't think I can ever put him in a box again." I know I won't lose the memories after we move, not really. But at least bringing some of my old things with me to our new place will help make the transition easier.

"I know you've never been great with change," Mom says. "Sadly, I think you get that from me."

I think of my dad, who's often a little too happy to

uproot everything and try something totally different. I guess too much change can be a bad thing sometimes, but not enough is bad, too. It makes you terrified of anything being different. Heck, it can even make you terrified of changing how you make cookies. And if I'm going to be a famous pastry chef one day, then those cookies need to be perfect, no matter how much change it takes.

"It's okay," I tell her. "I think I'm finally figuring out the right amount."

Acknowledgments

Hugely enormous thanks to my husband and to my family, to my writer and non-writer friends, to everyone at The Writers' Loft, to Aubrey Poole and the team at Sourcebooks, and to Ammi-Joan Paquette. I can't thank you all enough, but I'll keep trying

Turn the page for a sneak preview of

The Gossip File

Book 3 in The Dirt Diary series

Available January 2015

Editor's note: The following is unedited and may change in the final book.

Chapter 1

Rachel, how many rocks did you put in this suitcase?"
Mom asks as she drags my luggage out of the back
of her dented minivan. Evan, my too-cute-for-words boyfriend, rushes over to help ease the ancient bag to the curb
in front of the airport terminal.

"Here you go, Booger Crap," Evan says as he brings the
bag to me.

I'm so used to his goofy nickname for me that I don't
even roll my eyes this time. Instead, I give a shy smile and
say, "Thanks."

When he grins back at me, his green eyes don't twinkle
like they usually do. We're both pretending that my being
away for two weeks won't be a big deal, but it stinks that
I'm leaving when things are finally good between us. Plus,
I think he's been gearing up to kiss me all week. But I guess
that will have to wait until I get back from visiting my dad

in Florida. I seriously doubt my first kiss is going to happen at the airport in front of my mom.

Oh my goldfish. What if that's what Evan is planning? My mom will *never* let me live that down! My hands are shaking as I grab the suitcase and hurry through the parking garage.

"Wait up!" Mom calls. I hear her and Evan's footsteps behind me, trying to keep up, but I don't slow down until I spot my best friend, Marisol, waiting at the airline check-in.

"Rachel!" she squeals, rushing toward me.

I can't believe how lucky I am that her parents agreed to let her come to Florida with me. If I had to do this trip by myself, no doubt I'd accidentally wind up in Omaha instead of Orlando.

"We're going to have so much fun!" she says.

Marisol's mom stands behind her, looking skeptical about that fact. "I checked the weather report in Florida this morning," she says. "It's going to be near a hundred degrees."

Marisol shrugs. "It was ninety here the other day. Besides, that's what air conditioning is for!"

Okay, Florida in the summer might not be ideal, but I've been dreaming of going there ever since my sixth birthday when my dad promised we'd visit Disney World one day.

Eight years later, I'm still excited to make that dream come true. Plus, with school starting in a few weeks, it'll be nice to finally get a vacation. I've spent all summer working for my mom's cleaning business, taking pastry classes, and organizing baking competitions (not to mention pulling pranks on people and making a general mess out of everything). It'll be a relief to hang out by the pool, spend some much-needed quality time with my dad, and relax. Who cares if it'll be a little hot?

Evan hangs back while we go check in at the airline counter. After Marisol and her mom are squared away, the ticket agent waves my mom and me forward without even looking up at us.

"What's your destination today?" he drones.

"Omaha," I blurt out, handing over the flight confirmation my mom gave me.

The man finally glances up at me. "What was that?"

"I mean Orlando," I say. "Orlando! Where SeaWorld is with all the whales!"

He raises an eyebrow and then looks at my mom. "And who's this?"

"I'm her mother," Mom jumps in. "I'll be escorting her to the gate, so I believe I'll need a pass to get through security."

The man takes her driver's license and studies it for a

long time. Then he looks at Mom again, and I can tell they're coming, the words that always make my stomach clench into a ball.

"She doesn't look like you," he says.

"She's my daughter," Mom says, putting a protective arm around me. "But she looks like her father. He's Korean."

The man nods, but I can tell he's still not sure about us. Does he think my mom stole me or something? Or that because I don't have blond hair like she does, that means we're trying to sneak her into the airport?

Just when I think my stomach might clench itself into a black hole, the man sighs and grabs my suitcase. Then he hands me an enormous badge that I have to wear around my neck. I realize Marisol has one too. The badges scream "UNACCOMPANIED MINORS FLYING ALONE" which is ridiculous since Marisol is more responsible than most adults I know.

Finally, we get to the security checkpoint. That means it's time to say good-bye to Evan.

As I shuffle over to him, it hits me that I haven't thought this dropping off at the airport plan through. When Evan volunteered to come along, I was excited that he wanted to see me off like a real boyfriend would. I didn't consider the fact that he's going to have to ride all the way back to his house alone with my mom. What on earth will they talk about?

"So," he says. "I guess you have to go now, huh?"

I nod. "They're going to start boarding soon."

"Well." He looks down at his sneakers. "Text me when you land so I know you got there, okay?"

"I will."

When he glances up at me, I suck in a breath. He has a total "I'm going to kiss you" look on his face. This is really going to happen!

But wait. My mom is *right there*. Even though she's talking to Marisol's mom and not looking in my direction—probably to give us some privacy—it still feels like her eyes are lasering into me.

Evan takes a step forward, and I start to panic. What do I do?

"If you need something to talk to my mom about on the way home," I blurt out, "ask her about music from when she was a kid. She won't stop babbling for hours."

Evan's forehead crinkles. "Okay. Thanks for the tip."

Gah! Why does this have to be so awkward? Why can't I be brave like Marisol? She'd kiss the guy and be done with it, no matter who was watching.

"Anyway," he adds. "Have fun. I'll—I'll miss you."

My face goes hot. "I'll miss you too," I whisper.

And then I feel it. Evan's face inching toward mine. The scent of peppermint on his breath and the heat off of his skin getting closer and closer. My mind goes blank for a second. I can't believe it. My first kiss is really going to happen…in front of my mom!

Just as Evan's lips are about to brush mine, I jerk my head sideways. All Evan's mouth finds is my ear.

Holy miniature marshmallows. Evan Riley tried to kiss me. And I turned away!

He coughs and steps back. "Um, so have fun," he says, his face flushing bright pink.

"I—I'm sorry. It's not…with everyone here…"

Why did my stupid head have to flinch? So what if my mom is right there? She's not even watching! This could have been the perfect moment, and I ruined it!

Maybe I can fix it. If I lean in and kiss him, then everything will be okay. *Do it*, I tell myself.

"Rachel!" Mom calls over her shoulder. "It's time to go."

The moment shatters like a dropped candy cane. Evan and I look at each other for a long second.

"I wish I didn't have to go," I say softly. "I wish…" If

only I could be the kind of person who doesn't care what people think, the kind who does what she wants. But I think that Rachel only exists in an alternate universe where everyone eats cupcakes for breakfast and never has to go to gym class.

"It's okay," Evan says, reaching out his finger to give my nose an affectionate tap. "Two weeks isn't that long."

I know he's right, but it still feels like I took our perfect airport good-bye and turned it on its ear. Literally.

I'm still shaking as we go through the security checkpoint. When we get to the gate, my mom pulls me into a hug and starts sobbing into my ear.

"Mom," I say meekly, trying to think of something comforting to say. I always freeze up when people get really emotional. "Um, at least there aren't any sharks in Orlando, so you don't have to worry about me being a shark attack victim, right?"

She lets out a little laugh and pulls away. "It's not even on the water," she says, wiping her eyes.

"Exactly. No sharks. So I'll be fine. Will *you* be okay?"

Mom nods as she keeps sniffling. "I'll have plenty to keep me busy with apartment hunting and all the new Ladybug Cleaners clients." She leans in and kisses the top of my head. "Don't worry about me. Just have fun with your dad."

I feel bad that Mom is going to be working her buttons off and looking for apartments for us while I'm on vacation, but I couldn't say no when my dad asked me to visit. Besides, it might be months before we actually sell our house, so I doubt Mom will find a new place without me.

"I love you," I whisper as I give her one last hug. If we draw this out any longer, I'm going to start crying too.

When Mom finally lets me go, I can't help peering back the way we came, even though Evan must be halfway across the airport by now.

I should feel like I'm at the start of an adventure. I should be excited to finally be leaving home and seeing my dad. But I can't help wishing I could have one more minute in my regular life before I go.

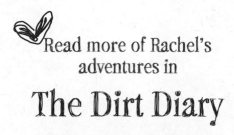

Read more of Rachel's
adventures in

The Dirt Diary

About the Author

Anna Staniszewski lives outside Boston with her wacky dog and her slightly less wacky husband. She was a Writer-in-Residence at the Boston Public Library and a winner of the PEN New England Discovery Award. When she's not writing, Anna teaches, reads, and avoids cleaning her house. Visit her at www.annastan.com.

Sedman Photography